ORION

Satan's Pride

by

A.G. Kirkham

Orion,
Copyright © 2020 AK Publishing

All rights reserved. No part of this book may be reproduced by any mechanical, photographic, or electronic process or in the form of phonographic recording; nor may it be stored in a retrieval system, transmitted, or otherwise copied for public or private use without the prior written permission of the author.

AK Publishing
Aurora, Ontario, Canada
www.romancebyagkirkham.com

Kirkham, A.G., 1965 –
Orion: Satan's Pride Series
A.G. Kirkham

Kate Studer, Editor
Franny Armstrong, Cover Design
Interior Layout, www.formatting4U.com

Printed and bound in the USA

ISBN 978-1-999-1311-3-5 (Paperback)
ISBN 978-1-999-1311-2-8 (eBook)

Note to the reader: This book is a work of fiction. The characters, organizations, events and places portrayed in this book are products of the author's imagination and are either fictitious or are used fictitiously. Any similarity to a real person, living or dead is purely coincidental and not intended by the author. The information is provided for entertainment and inspirational purposes only. In the event, you use any of the information in this book for yourself, which is your constitutional right, the author and publisher assumes no responsibility for your actions.

Contents

Acknowledgments i
Chapter 1: Mine for Tonight 1
Chapter 2: How Do I Let the Past Go 9
Chapter 3: The Things I'll Miss 13
Chapter 4: Where are you hiding? 21
Chapter 5: In this moment you can change your destiny 27
Chapter 6: Operation "Find the Fire" 35
Chapter 7: The Shocking Debrief 39
Chapter 8: Meeting of the Minds................. 47
Chapter 9: Diamond not Teflon 53
Chapter 10: Lady Pride Members take a stand .. 59
Chapter 11: Give and take 65
Chapter 12: Soft and slow 73
Chapter 13: Pink Glitter 81
Chapter 14: We'll make it perfect! 91
Chapter 15: Revolving Door 97
Chapter 16: Moving on 115
Chapter 17: Let me love you 123
Chapter 18: Bratty Brother 129
Chapter 19: The chair 137
Chapter 20: Orion will come 143

Chapter 21: Gabriella's Arrival 151
Chapter 22: Guard/Gabriella 155
Chapter 23: A Lifetime 161
Chapter 24: Cheap shot, Dad. 167
Chapter 25: Hanna 179
Chapter 26: They don't leave 181
Chapter 27: The Wedding 185
Chapter 28: The Ring 195
About Th e Author 199
Playlist for Orion's Book 200

Acknowledgments

To my family (Rick, Giulia, Antonio, Daniel, Samantha, Luca, Lia and Mila) thank you for always believing in me; to my dear friend Deborah, you give me hope and clarity, you mean the world to me. You have all been my inspiration and whose consistent support and optimism helped make this dream come true.

To my wonderful inspiration for Vi, Thank you Roxy. I am so grateful to know you. I hope I have represented the spunk and courage you show in all that you do.

Thank you, Franny Armstrong, for the beautiful book jacket. Your hard work and extreme patience is greatly appreciated.

To all of you that jumped in and assisted me in seeing this book through until it was perfect, I want to sincerely tell you how much you are appreciated.

CHAPTER 1

Mine for Tonight

Vi

I peer into those eyes. Those incredibly beautiful, smoke grey eyes. Filled with desire and torment. Both emotions fighting for priority. He fills me completely as I descend on his cock. One firm arm guides me down, yet wraps gently around my ribs, taking care to not aggravate my recent injury.

I was still recovering from the brutal attack of a madman who had set his sights on my dear friend Maddie. I'd walked into the studio, definitely at the wrong time and the deviant had decided to take his frustration out on me, in an attempt to lure Maddie out of her hiding hole, an escape room that War had built just for this occasion. The madman's plan was to lure Maddie out and put her through the same beating I was taking. Thank God it backfired. Dear sweet Maddie found the strength to fight back and came out prepared to confront him. And after seeing what he was doing to me, she shot him dead.

My Orion, even if it had only been for a few more days, had seen me at my worst possible state, both in mind and body. Since that moment I had felt him pulling back, pulling away from me, from us. In truth, he had been pulling away for the past six months but since the attack, he had been void. That's as close a word I can find to describe him. Our moments alone were tender, loving, even sweet.

Here in this bed, when we are together like this, I feel him connected to me and know beyond a shadow of a doubt that this is where I am meant to be.

I tip my head down so that our lips are a whisper apart. I love the soft touch of his lips against mine. We are both panting heavily; my body feels so complete with his cock stroking in and out in a rhythmic euphoria. I love the fullness of how he feels inside me, filling me. How he tastes when I lick his lips and catch the hint of scotch mixed with his manly freshness.

I am so close. I can't hold off any longer. My muscles tense and contract around his massive cock. I want to slow down, but I can't. I want to keep him here, inside me. Orion moans, sounding more like a snarl and a growl as he inches closer to his release as well.

"Vi, get there," he urges. His eyes are wild with need and intensity. His hands grip my waist tighter, noting that my climax is imminent. I continue to hold off my orgasm as long as I can. Orion takes his finger and begins circling my clit. That is all I can handle; a moan erupts as Orion smothers his mouth over mine in a long, wet, sensual kiss. Dueling tongues and tiny nips at my lips and neck as he finds his own release. I watch intently, loving the beauty of all that is Orion when he lets go. I am not going to last, so I take in the show. All of it mesmerizing, every movement, sound and touch. So good, so right.

I know his eyes will turn in the next moment. They'll go back to his cold steel grey. Impassive. Immoveable. I hitch my breath, gearing up for the disconnect. His eyes open, and there it is. The guarded expression has arisen once again, shutting me out.

Orion is still gentle with me as he lifts me up and off his body, placing me gently on the bed beside him. He climbs out of our bed, saunters into the bathroom off to the side of the bedroom, and moments later, reappears to clean me up. His movements are tender, even loving. After having tossed the facecloth back into the bathroom, uncaring if it hit the sink or floor, he climbs back in beside me, tucking me close into his side. He rearranges the sheets and covers to cocoon me. Wrapped in his safe warmth.

All these actions say love. The tenderness, the way he's holding me, is so sweet. I can almost convince myself that he is emotionally here with me. Not just a body seeking my warmth. Of course, as usual, I make the mistake of paying closer attention. I feel the stiffness of his stature. His arm is tense around my waist, and the ever-present silence that follows our love making vibrates across the walls and settles into my soul. It is a slow retreat into himself. It hurts that I feel this so intensely, right into the very core of me.

At one time, I'd convinced myself that this would

ease, lessen with time, and we would grow together as we became more in tune with one another. I thought as our relationship evolved so would his behavior to better represent our union. At first, there were small changes. They lifted my spirits and I became more confident that he was becoming more relaxed with me. He smiled more when he was around me. He would spend the night after sex and hold me all night long. Everything was moving forward, just as it should, like normal couples, becoming more connected to one another in a normal relationship.

We laughed together to the point that my side ached, my cheeks hurt, and I was blessed to hear the roar of his laughter in return. He had a tendency to take an unruly curl and trace it behind my ear. His touch made me tingle all the way to my toes. We had reached the point where we had sets of clothes at each other's apartments; basically, wasting money by not amalgamating our possessions and picking a place to live together. I didn't point this out. I convinced myself that I was giving him time to come to that realization on his own. I was sure he was headed where I was, and since he was the kind of man who liked to come to his own conclusions, I thought to let him get there on his own.

Glancing over my shoulder, I am reminded of his sheer beauty. A giant of a man. A human formed bear. They call him Orion, the hunter, and I have also adopted to calling him that, although, I think a more fitting name would be Grizzly. He is a huge mountain of a man, being over six feet tall and built like a first-class wrestler. Thick legs and thick arms. His chest is a hundred percent pure muscle. He is magnificent. His face is bearded and has been since he was a teenager. He told me that he never looked like a kid and never wanted to, hence his decision to let the beard grow. I tease him, calling it fur. His hair is tousled with dark curls and a very light touch of grey gathering on the sides. This is the man I always dreamed of being with. My dream man. I fell in love with him at the first crook of his finger; trying to get my attention to order his first meal at Molly's Place, the diner I work at. I knew he was my one.

Orion walked in very early that first morning we met. It was so early that there were still morning dew drops glistening on the grass as the sun rose. I always loved the early shift. I got to see the sun come up and meet the most amazing people who had stopped by to visit our town. Some only stopped for the hour to refuel their bodies and get back on the road to where they were heading. Some stayed for longer visits, taking in the country charm, while others decided this is where they belonged and stayed forever. That's how I landed here.

Orion, Guard, and War were in that morning, almost three years ago. I was sure they were the type to refuel and take off. I was behind that counter, having just perked the first pot of coffee and I'd laid out the fresh bagels, breads, muffins and other treats that had just arrived when the bell tinkled above the door. Guard led the way. My heart stopped. I thought he was absolutely gorgeous. War followed close behind and I thought heaven walked in; two hotties in my presence. I felt like I'd hit the hot guy lottery. Then something happened that made the world cease to exist; I heard and saw nothing except my grizzly bear

ORION

strutting into Molly's. He was sublime, and I knew then that I was meant to be with him and him with me.

They were men of few words. They ordered, ate, and hung about, talking amongst themselves. I was completely disillusioned that Orion would even notice my mere existence, they were so engrossed in their own conversation.

My chat with the guys extended as far as taking their orders, casual "thank you" for each of them, and my nonchalant dropping by to refill their coffee cups. I was sure to give the rest of my regulars just as much attention, especially my table of older men who'd congregated to discuss their next fishing trip. After a few hours, the hot bikers paid their tab, leaving a generous tip and I watched them saunter out the door. I did nothing. I just let Orion walk out, without doing a damn thing to stop him. There he was, my one and only, and I let him slip away. I began to chastise myself, remembering that I always allowed life to lead me through. I kept waiting for something special to happen to me, instead of making it happen.

I was not an unhappy person. In fact, I was probably one of the most positive and cheery people you might meet. I loved people, life, and experiences. I enjoyed making friends and getting to know all the regulars at Molly's. I loved to learn through new experiences, loved listening to the amazing stories that came out through conversations. I had a great apartment above the diner that I fixed up to reflect my personality—an awesome place to live, a great job where I got to meet the most interesting visitors, even if the money was modest, but I didn't care because I was an awesome waitress and made decent tips. I made extra money by designing unique jewelry and it made for great extra income and was only becoming more popular. I was happy, creative, and fun-loving. The only elusive factor was that person to share my life with.

I watched him leave. I sighed and decided maybe the love gods were against this union, maybe it wasn't meant to be. I continued with my routine throughout the day, thinking how lucky I was to have met three handsome men that day. Seize the positive!

As the day wound down, I decided to treat myself to some ice cream. I rarely splurged on my love of ice cream simply because I believe in being healthy. Treats are awesome but all things in moderation. I was already working out at the local gym an hour a day and ate healthy, I am not giving up my indulgences but I do reel myself in to stay in a healthy place. Compromising my wellbeing was something I wasn't willing to do. I wanted to be healthy and stay strong, but I certainly did not want to be a freak about it. I'm definitely not a gym bunny.

I was lucky that my shift ended while the sun was still shining, another one of the perks of working the early shift. Stepping into the sunshine, I found myself eye to eye with my grizzly. He was leaning against his Harley. One foot braced forward, arms crossed in front of his large body, with a gleam in his eyes as he stared right at me. I blinked, then blinked again. I was sure I was imagining things. My breath hitched.

I moved closer to the curb, towards his bigger than life presence. Even the street looked small with his bike and body taking up more room than I thought possible.

ORION

I wanted to say something clever and under normal circumstances, I would never be at a loss for words. I worked in customer service; I was always able to chat. Yet there I was with the most alluring man I had ever had the good fortune to set my sights on, and nothing even remoting interesting to say entered my mind, despite my hoping to sound clever and cute. Instead, crickets! Gaaah! So frustrating! All I could do was stare at all his goodness.

Orion finally broke the silence. "Prettiest little thing I've ever seen. That's what I thought when I first set eyes on you," he quirked.

I let his words sink in. I took a breath, and then another. "Hey," I said breathily.

"Hey," Orion replied, as a smirk spread across his face. It was then that I knew I would give anything to have him smile at me each day, forever spending my time with him.

I finally found words, "Want to grab and ice cream?" I asked and he responded with laughter that spanned his face.

My feelings swing back to the here and now, this moment with his arm wrapped solidly around my waist, his even breath blowing gently against the crook of my neck. I will cherish this moment and keep it entrenched in my memory as I have all the moments that led to this one. These times will be all I have to remember him by.

CHAPTER 2

How Do I Let the Past Go

Orion

The compound is close to empty. I look around the room to notice all the changes that have been made since Ava appeared on the scene. The place is filled with an array of furniture. Large black leather couches with side tables, along with sturdy armchairs that match, are strewn around the main living area. Since Ava, Maddie and Vi have been with the Pride, lately very often, the hint of a woman's touch graces the compound. The glasses are nicer, and the chipped stuff has been thrown out. There are bowls for the chips and salsa. Apparently only animals eat out of bags and jars.

My sight transfers to the blue chair that was bought especially for Vi after the beat down she received from that fucker, Jeffrey. He slammed his fist into my woman's face and ribs and kicked her repeatedly until she was bloody and broken, all because she would not call out for Maddie. Vi was loyal to the core refusing to give up her friend. I didn't see it happen, but the results are forever imprinted in my brain. They haunt my thoughts. I still have nightmares about that tragic day.

I was running into the room when we heard the shots being fired. My first thought upon entering the room was that Jeffery had shot Vi with all the blood surrounding her. I was never more scared, and never have I felt more helpless in my life. I pulled her into my arms. I called her name over and over with no response. I was terrified that she wouldn't make it. I heard the ambulance coming but time seemed to slow to a crawl as I waited for them to attend to Vi.

I kept my hand on her pulse. As long as it kept beating, I would be fine. I blame myself. I didn't protect her well enough. She wasn't supposed to be there that day. I should have kept closer watch on her.

History repeated itself, only this time I was in the country and present and still couldn't protect the woman I loved. I've lost one woman and child because I wasn't around and now that I am here, I came close to losing Vi. How could I even think to take our relationship further? My father wasn't a role model. Let's say it how it is, he's a dick. I left to salvage the man I wanted to become, and I am still falling short.

"Where is your head at?" I hear Risk's rough voice penetrate my thoughts. I turn to look at him, tearing my eyes from the chair. "You keep staring at

HOW DO I LET THE PAST GO

that chair, man. It ain't going anywhere and she isn't sitting in it anymore," he finishes.

I try and remain stoic. I am known for being the self-controlled brother. The one who thinks things through. I am informed, strategic and calculated in my thought process. This is what my crew needs from me, and what I need to be. So, I am controlled. Always.

"I'm good, brother," I say in a firm tone, not giving anything away.

"Then why do you look like someone stole your bike?" Risk teases, handing me a beer as he takes a swig of his.

"Some motherfucker steals my bike; I would not be sitting here having a chat with you. I would be tracking their ass down and giving them the pounding, they deserve," I retort, meaning every single word.

CHAPTER 3

The Things I'll Miss

Vi

Walking into Hanna's Bakery brings a small smile to my lips. One that has been virtually nonexistent for the last while. Hanna's place is small and quaint. She recently opened a little seating area because the masses in town have been begging for her to make her baked goods more readily available. She used to only take custom orders for parties or for Molly's. Hanna is adorable and greets me with a shy smile and a wave. She has her regular uniform on, oversized jeans and a t-shirt, with plain white sneakers. Her caramel brown hair is in her usual loose-hanging ponytail. I know that she is very self-conscious of her body because is well endowed both in the booty and the breasts, with warm soft brown eyes and a coy smile, she has no idea how pretty she is. The best thing about Hanna is that she is one hundred percent thrilled that I walked through the door to indulge in the delicious goodness she takes so much pride in making. She is always so happy when someone comes in to visit her. She is as genuine as they come.

Lately, I have been craving her lemon zest squares. Those tangy lemon layer over the cinnamon swirl crust is magnificent. So decadent that I just can't help myself. I'll miss those squares and Hanna's sweet smile. I walk up to the counter and somehow, she already knows exactly what I want as she places one in a lilac dessert dish with pale blue flowers decorating the edges. Those are the colours she chose as her main theme for her bakery. She has the walls painted in pale blue and one accent wall in lilac with beautiful glass dessert stands on display, featuring an array of specialty bars, tarts, cupcakes, cakes, and more. Hanna decides a week in advance what she will bake based on a blackboard easel she set up so her recurring customers could add their requests. She has a following because she listens, and she makes everything with care and love.

"Hey doe eyes," I say. She lets out a little giggle and quirks her head slightly to her shoulder. "Will you please box half a dozen of my squares for me?" Lately, I have been unable to keep anything down and the only thing that seems to do it for me is those lemon squares. Crazy but true, so against my norm I am taking some to go and have my one a day, like a vitamin.

"Half a dozen?" she asks excitedly. "Are you meeting up with Ava and Maddie?" Hanna knows how close we girls are and that we often meet up for coffee and dessert. We manage to talk the afternoon away, solving the world's problems—from our perspective, of course.

"Nope. Those are all for me." I reply, as I lick my lips with anticipation.

"I can make you fresh ones tomorrow. As a matter of fact, you can come by every day for a fresh lemon square. I'll make them just for you, Vi," Hanna says happily.

"No, honey, these will do," I respond solemnly. I come to realize that these will be the last I will ever have and their taste needs to last me for forever. Maybe I should get a dozen and I can freeze a few.

"Are you okay, Vi?" She looks at me intently, seeming concerned. "You look a little pale, sweetie, and you have been super quiet lately. If you ever want to talk, I'm a very good listener and I will never tell a soul. I keep my promises and will keep your secrets," she says, then shrugs her shoulders and adds, "Besides, I have no one to tell."

I see her worry is sincere. She wears her emotions like a beacon in a storm. Then a crack in my hard shell happens. Maybe, it's because I have been holding it all in for fear of coming completely apart. Or because my hormones are all over the place. Whatever the reason, I find myself falling completely apart as tears flow freely down my cheeks. Hanna immediately winds around the counter, freeing her hands of the dish she was readying for me and takes me into her warm embrace. She lets me sob softly into her shoulder as she leads me down a hallway and through a backroom that leads into her home after placing "back in five" sign on the door. She guides me gently onto her sofa and sits next to me, whispering quiet words of comfort.

I am unsure of how long I sit with her. I finally gather myself together and get some control over my emotions. "Thank you, Hanna. I shouldn't be taking you away from the front. You have a business to run," I say as I wipe away the tears and attempt to scramble out of my seat. She reaches out a hand to stop me and keeps me in place beside her while still holding on.

"How far along are you, Vi?" she asks softly. Her voice is calm and soothing.

I whip my head up to meet her eyes. "How did you know?" I inquire, completely confused over how she'd come to this conclusion. I mean, I'm not showing yet and my two dearest friends, who see me all the time, haven't figured it out or suspected.

"Vi, I have two sisters and one sister-in-law who've produced a combined six nieces and nephews. My sisters would cry at a puppy video on YouTube or fall apart when I made their favorite cookies. This always happened to one of them when they were expecting a little miracle," she tells me. Hanna is calling my sweet baby a miracle. I have been feeling so scared and alone that I haven't given myself the time or luxury to consider what a gift I have been blessed with.

Reality and panic quickly take over. "No one knows, Hanna. You can't say anything. I'm begging you," I plead with her, squeezing her hand. I can't have anyone involved. It would create so much conflict.

She covers my hands, stating firmly, "I won't say anything." She looks stricken that I would suggest such a thing. "I would never take that joy away from you. It's your news to tell and I want you to have the pleasure of sharing it."

"I'm not telling anyone," I state stoically.

"Vi, please think about this. A baby is a beautiful thing," she says, tightening the grip on my hand laying in my lap.

I realize that she believes I'm going to abort the pregnancy. I look up sharply, "Oh no! I'm planning on keeping the baby." I hear her sigh of relief and continue, "But I am leaving town to start over someplace else," I say in defeat. I gulp down more tears; my lower lip begins to tremble, and fresh tears begin their descent.

Hanna blinks in confusion. "What are you saying? Orion needs to know that he's going to be a dad. And Maddie and Ava love you so much and are going to be great aunties to this little one. They will all be here to support you and give you the time and care you need. They will want to enjoy this time with you and celebrate all the amazing stages like planning of a baby shower and…" Her voice trails off as she sees me shaking my head.

"No, Hanna. I am counting on you to keep this to yourself. Orion never wanted to be a father and lately, he has been distancing himself from me. He's more removed than ever. I can see him drifting further and further away from me. I love him too much to use this baby to keep him with me. But I don't want to live without my child and that means I need to leave him," I tell her sadly as fresh tears cloud my vision. "I've hoped for a long time that he would want to have a family, Hanna. I brought up the subject a couple of times. I tell him how great he is with Gavin and how

Gavin adores his time with Uncle O. But Orion says he's not meant to be a dad. He said that he grew up hating his dad and didn't want that to happen to him." I catch my breath. "Please, Hanna, this cannot be repeated."

"Please, Vi, think this through. Where will you go?" Hanna's voice is strained.

"I don't know," I reply with a heavy sigh. I really have no idea where I will end up at this point. "I haven't figure that out yet."

"How will you support yourself and the baby?" she asks. I can see that she's stressing about the entire situation. "You can't be out there all by yourself."

"I began an online jewelry business a while back and it's making good headway. I also have some money saved up and I hope to find another job waiting tables until the baby is born to help me through until the business becomes a fulltime option," I relay, taking in a heavy breath. I am proud of the fact that I have formulated a plan. Although I would prefer that Orion was part of the equation and could be excited about our baby and so I could live here with him forever.

"You have an online jewelry business? I had no idea!" she exclaims incredulously.

"Yeah. Some of the stores in town carry my pieces as well as some other small shops in neighboring towns. I am getting more traction and traffic to my website and the orders are increasing. It's been slow but it is building. The tricky part is managing my time, balancing making the jewelry with working to increase sales by marketing my line and with working at the diner and eventually with raising a baby. I've been taking care of myself for a long time,

THE THINGS I'LL MISS

Hanna. My mom left me with my grandparents when her new beau decided he didn't want a kid around. I don't want my baby dealing with their father leaving them. Orion didn't want to be a dad and I won't force my baby on him, just to have to leave us later," I confess. As I say this, I am feeling overwhelmed. Hanna stares off. I can tell that she is mulling over all the information I have dropped in her lap. After a long, thoughtful pause, Hanna makes her move.

"Vi, if I become a short term investor in your business, just to see you through until you are making the income you need to make it your fulltime career, then you won't need to work another job," she says innocently. She's a sneaky little thing, trying to make an "investment" that translates into charity.

"What you're really saying is that you are going to give me money until I'm on my feet, but I will tell you right now that I don't want charity, Hanna," I say fiercely.

"No, no, Vi. Hear me out. I want to lend you money and you will pay it back when your business is solid and completely viable. You can pay me back whenever you can, and you can add interest if you want but this way you can concentrate on the business and the baby. This will save you money in childcare," she says as I shake my head firmly, but Hanna pushes through. "Listen, Vi, a good mom puts her baby's needs before her pride." And just like that, Hanna has me.

I perk my head up. "I am not going to be a bad mom," I say emphatically.

"No, you're not. Because you are going to stay in my home in Pickward County, just outside of town. You will set up a room for your business and raise your baby," she says happily, clapping her hands in excitement.

"I can't..." I begin.

"You can, and you will since I want to help you and you need to have someone to rely on, if only for a little while. And truly, Vi, I want to," she says quietly. "It would be an honor to know that you trust me enough to let me help."

Just like that, Hanna and I became more than acquaintances and a friendship is formed. We sit and plan how it would work including the interest payments, which takes a long while as Hanna is insisting it isn't necessary. I eat my squares and for the first time in months, I don't feel completely alone.

I will miss my friends, whom I consider sisters. Maddie and Ava are so important to me and I wish I could let them know my plans. I think of telling them, time and time again, however I know that I will be placing them in an awkward position since their men are Satan's Pride members. Guard, Ava's husband is the President and War is engaged to Maddie; he is the enforcer. When they are asked questions, they will be forced to lie, and I will be the reason for their secrets. I refuse to come between them and their men.

I will miss my job at Molly's, where I engage in daily banter with my regulars. Listening to Joe and his pals making plans for their next big catch at the lake. I will miss looking at the door where my love first walked in. I will miss the man I love far more. I find solace in knowing that I will always have a piece of him with me when my baby arrives.

CHAPTER 4

Where are you hiding?

Orion

One month later

She hasn't called, texted, or emailed. She hasn't made a move to contact me at all. She hasn't responded to any of my attempts to contact her. I was anguished over the thought of her being taken by a rival MC to torture me. I imagined the most horrible things being done to her. Then I found out she walked away from me, her friends, and all her family—from the club.

I am not sure which is worse. I'd never want Vi to hurt, but the idea of her walking away from everything we had without a word guts me.

After twelve consecutive phone calls, and an

endless number of text messages, I ran to her apartment, worried she was sick and couldn't call for help. I remember walking into her apartment above the diner at Molly's and finding it empty. Her clothes were gone, her pictures, everything. The apartment was desolate and cold. I cornered Molly, the owner, and she was as stunned as the rest of us. At least Vi had the decency to write Molly a note. It read:

"*Molly,*

I am so sorry that I'm leaving you without giving you any notice. I didn't know how else to make a clean break. I appreciate all that you have done for me. I hope that you continue to think of me fondly.
Love,
Vi"

I went to see Ava and grilled her until Guard had enough and stepped in, shoving me out of the room. "What the fuck is wrong with you?" he roared. "If she knew anything, she would tell you. Can't you see that she is losing her mind with worry?" He was fuming mad, gritting his teeth. Guard is my best friend but there is no way he would allow anything to happen to Ava. He continued his lecture. "The question is, why did she go? If you find out why she left, then maybe we can figure out where she might be." Guard calmed his voice, but I was too pissed and hurt to hear him out.

"She left because she had enough of what I had to offer. Probably found something better and moved on.

She left because she was a coward and couldn't face me to break it off," I screamed, right in his face.

Ava came storming into the room and pulled me down by the collar, forcing me to bend so that we were nose to nose and toe to toe. This was no small feat considering she was five-foot-four compared to my six-foot-four frame. My eyes met hers.

"Vi is anything but weak. If she left, she had a good reason. I am terrified for her; Guard is terrified for her. Maddie is going insane, calling and texting every five minutes in the hopes that she will answer. The Club misses her and respects her and all you are thinking of is your own pain. I am sorry to say this, but you pushed her away. She tried so hard to make you see all of her and all she had to offer, and you picked and chose when and where you would include her in your life. She wanted you to love her as she deserved to be loved and you failed," she spewed venomously.

I jolted back in horror. It was like a slap in the face. I didn't love her like she deserved to be loved.

I left without a word then rode for hours. I stepped off my bike when I got to the only place I could find quiet. Away from the rest of the crew, where I can be at complete peace. Although I love my brothers and would lay down my life for each and every one of them, I've never found the serenity that I find when I am here.

Guard knows that I lost them both. My Lisa and the baby she was carrying. I was on a military tour in Afghanistan. I remember the letter I received from Lisa informing me that we were having a baby. I was going to be a father. She begged me to look after myself and to come home safe. We were in seclusion for six months without outside communication, on a special mission. Risk was in my unit. He made the day bearable. He and I would talk about going home; he was going to be my kid's godfather. We had been through so much together and with all the shit in the world, I thought my baby would be the purest form of our friendship I could offer him.

When I got back to base, I was called into the office and was told that Lisa had been killed during a robbery. She was at the wrong place at the wrong time. She had gone to the bank to cash the check I sent her when a thief came running out. In his fit of panic, he pulled the trigger. Her life and that of our child was gone—just like that. Our plans for the future ended because of one man's bad choices. I came home to a cemetery plot. I lost everything. Pain ripped through me, and I vowed I would never let that happen to me again. Yet here I am, feeling an even deeper pain than I have ever felt. I let Vi into my life, I got too close, and now she's gone. I come here to the cemetery to talk to Lisa whenever I need to work things through.

This is where I met Guard, all those years ago. He came to the cemetery week after week to see me. I was drowning in grief. He walked me through the pain. Gave me a purpose to help me keep moving forward, introduced me to a bunch of great, honest men, who would have my back and appreciated my talents from the military. Being a technical guru, I can find information that most cannot. I have a knack, a talent—some say a gut sense. That makes me the informed, controlled thinker. So why can't I find Vi?

Here I sit again, this time alone. I don't find quiet or answers. I feel cold, empty and lost without her.

WHERE ARE YOU HIDING?

My mission was to keep Vi safe. The MC has had their fair share of turbulent storms and I wanted to keep her out of it all. I thought she knew what she meant to me, how much I cared for her. I didn't say those three words, but didn't she know I was just keeping her away from enemy eyes? I never made her my Old Lady, but everyone knew she was claimed by me. I figure if I never formally gave her the title, the other MCs wouldn't notice her, and it would make her less of a target. Instead, she misread the meaning behind my actions and left me.

Vi left me because I wasn't enough for her. Well fuck her then! There are plenty of women who will take what I'm willing to give them.

Where are you hiding, Vi? Guess it doesn't matter anymore.

CHAPTER 5

In this moment you can change your destiny

Hanna

Maddie and Ava have been so awesome and generous in assisting me in growing my business, placing orders at every opportunity. My special, made-to-order theme-based cakes have graced their tables countless times. They have ordered sweets tables filled with desserts for every event they, or the Club, holds. I sometimes think that they invent reasons to have me bring over desserts just so they can feast. I never would have thought that MC men would have such sweet tooths, but they all hover around the dessert table and inhale the goodness. Maybe this club should be referred to as Sugar Binge instead of Satan's Pride. Ava and Maddie have become friendly with me and I am happy to know that they like to include me in their coffee dates from time to time. Most of the time, I make an excuse. I feel ridiculous next those beautiful women. Here I am Miss Plain Jane amongst a rock star, and dancer. Funny really.

This weekend the MC has asked me to provide them with an array of goodies. Ava tells me that the guys have been really shaken by Vi's absence and Orion has been awful to be around. He has taken to drinking himself into oblivion. I am so sad that he is going through this. Vi is no better off. When she thinks I'm not looking, I see her shed tears. I wish they would just sit and talk it out. I guess that would be hard to do since she is hidden away pretty well, thanks to me. For tonight, I am happy to drop off the pastries, cookies, macaroons, brownies and lemon squares. Then I need to check on Vi before I go to bed tonight.

She is over three months along and she has been violently ill practically every day since the day she came to see me. I know that the pregnancy is a huge part of it, but I think that she misses Orion so much that she's making herself sick. I dropped in to see her last week and noticed how much weight she's lost. It's very concerning. I suggested that she schedule an earlier appointment with her doctor. She was having trouble concentrating on her designs. Her baby bump is protruding. Despite the weight loss and tossing her cookies daily, she gently rubs her baby bump and has talks with him or her. It's super cute.

I park in front of the back doors and pop the trunk open. Immediately my car is swarmed by a team of

IN THIS MOMENT YOU CAN CHANGE YOUR DESTINY

four prospects. Handsome young men, all looking to be patched and solid members of Satan's Pride. They would have to be, from what I hear. They do not condone disloyalty and unfairness. Risk comes out to supervise and damn he looks good—too good. He makes me rethink my vow of staying away from men. I decided after my disaster of a marriage, which I am still trying to end, that men only want to use women like me. The last man almost did me in physically and mentally. I know that I do not hold the same appeal as women like elegant Ava, beautiful Maddie, or spunky and resilient Vi. What would anyone want with a frumpy baker?

    I shake those thoughts out of my head and make my way to the tables that have been erected and are waiting for me to set out the sweet treats. I dress the table with a glossy back tablecloth and begin setting up the desserts. Hurrying myself along, I want to get out of here before the party becomes a little too rambunctious and rowdy. Maddie and Ava make their way over to say hello, eyeing the newly dressed table. Their eyes light up as they see the assortment.

    "Hi ladies. Do you like?" I ask and float my hand from one end of the table to the other, honing my inner Vanna White.

    "Dear God, Hanna, you have out done yourself. I may be spending most of my time right here." Ava giggles, reaching out to grab a chocolate macadamia cookie.

    "You are making it difficult for me to keep my fitness goals in check with all this glory in front of me," Maddie chimes in, reaching for a vanilla and strawberry swirl cake-pop. "I just don't care. These are my favorites," Maddie declares as she takes a nibble. I knew they were her favorite; that's why I made them. Seeing her enjoy the bite with a moan of pleasure, I can't help but smile along with them.

A movement from the corner of my right eye grabs my attention. I turn instinctively to see what's happening. It's Orion and Risk. They're arguing about something.

"What the fuck, brother? Give me back my drink," Orion booms, his hand exploding in the air.

"I think you've drunk enough to last you a month, asshole. It's time you start thinking with an uncluttered mind," Risk replies calmly.

"Are you saying that I'm letting the Pride down? That I'm letting the brothers down? That I'm not pulling my weight?" Orion volleys with a nasty sneer. He's mad, like really mad.

"No, man, that ain't it. You are taking unnecessary chances for no reason at all," Risk says firmly. He's not backing down either.

"Fine, keep the glass. I'll find some pussy instead," he says, turning back to add, "Or is that going to be a problem for you too?" He is drunk and acting stupid. So very stupid.

"What about Vi? You aren't thinking straight, Orion." Risk plants himself in front of Orion. "Stop and think!" he shouts, losing his temper.

"*Vi Left Me!*" Orion bellows. He accentuates each word with disgust. Or maybe that's just hurt disguised as hate.

I watch him walk over to two sluts—and I only call them that because Ava is right beside me, seeing the same scene, and calls them so. They are wanna-be bikers chicks who are willing to sleep with any and potentially all of the brothers. Unfortunately for them, the men in this Club may entertain them sexually, but never take them seriously.

Orion plunks himself in an armchair and hoists one woman on each of his knees. One begins to caress his chest and the other makes a move to kiss him, but he moves his head so that she nuzzles his neck. This is wrong. So very, very wrong. He's making a big mistake.

My feet drag me in front of Orion and my mouth has a mind of its own. I can't seem to control or stop myself.

"Orion, please don't do this. Please, I am asking you not to do this," I urge in a hushed tone, so that I'm not overheard by anyone else in the MC.

"What's it to you, sugar-girl?" he asks, then leans in to add suggestively, "You want in on this?"

I am taken aback for a moment. An indignant gasp escapes me. Good thing I bounce back quickly and formulate my thoughts to find a different method of reaching him.

"Orion, Vi would forgive you anything—anything, but what you are about to do. This she will never be able to forget or forgive. Is it worth the risk?" I ask with a defined tone. I am thinking is the wrong thing to say when Orion jolts out of his seat.

Orion stands, not caring that the women, who were just moments ago seated in his lap, are tossed to the floor with the intensity of his movement. He bends his large frame to meet my eyes. "What do you know about what Vi wants?" he spits out. Then, in a mere matter of seconds, as if the haze lifts from his clouded head, the light dawning on the horizon, he takes a menacing step forward, forcing me to move back a step. He quirks his head to the side to study me. "What do you know, Hanna?" Orion questions, with fury in his tone.

"I really think that she loves you and this would be the one thing that she would never be able to forgive you for," I reply softly. My eyes dart around, looking for an exit. Old instincts start to kick in. Instead I find myself surrounded by Ava, Maddie, Risk, War, and Orion, their eyes all staring at me intently. Damn me and my big mouth.

The bark of Orion's voice jolts me back to him. "How do you know that she loves me? She left me. Apparently, she didn't love me enough to stand by me. Found better and left." Orion states with anguish in his voice.

I can't help myself. My big mouth just keeps at it. Vi would never run off with someone else and his insinuation just makes me so very mad. I lose my temper.

"That's not true, you big oaf!", I yell. Yes, I am yelling at a man twice my size, which I immediately regret when he steps closer and grabs my upper arms. Oh Shit! My mom would be so mad right now to know that I was cussing, even if it is in my head.

"You know where she is," Orion announces with authority. His gaze is fixed on me and I can do nothing but stare into his distraught face. He continues, "You know where she is, and you know why she left. And I wanna know why she picked you to tell," he says. I am too dazed to say anything, so Orion gives me a little shake to knock me out of my stupor.

IN THIS MOMENT YOU CAN CHANGE YOUR DESTINY

I have been through much worse than this and no way am I betraying my friend's trust. I continue to look at him but say nothing.

Risk comes to stand by his side. He leans into Orion, placing a firm hand on his shoulder. "Stand down, man. We do not grab women the way you just did. Let her go, or I will have to make you." Risk holds true to his word and knocks Orion's hands away without giving him the opportunity to do it himself.

Orion faces off with Risk. "Who the fuck is your brother? You choose to stand up for a bitch who's keeping shit from me, from us, rather than helping me?," he bellows. He is so loud that the entire room comes to a standstill.

With a heavy sigh, Risk puts his hand back on Orion's shoulder. "We are brothers and brothers don't let brothers do something they will later regret, especially when their mind is influenced by massive amounts of alcohol. You want to know more? Then ask her. Don't put your hands on her," he says calmly and continues, "You know I'm right. Do not lose this opportunity."

I watched with sadness at the suffering in his eyes. Orion missed his beautiful redhead, his vibrant pixie with emerald green eyes. I can understand his desire for her. Vi is athletic and fit. She works hard, loves passionately, and cares deeply. She is only five-foot-four, but she packs a wallop in attitude and intelligence. He misses all of that. He may be a giant but his heart aches.

"Orion, Vi did not leave you because you weren't enough. She left because she is scared that she is not enough to keep you. I think you are both full of crap.

If you both would just sit down and talk it out and I mean really talk, you will guide yourselves back to one another. But, if you do what you were just planning on doing, there's no coming back from that." I turn to leave, then turn back to face him. "Vi says that you are the best tracker in the group. Have you really been looking?" I ask inquisitively. But soon realize that this too is a mistake. I've offended him again.

Orion shakes with fury. "Of course, I've been looking!" he exclaims indignantly.

I don't want the situation to get out of control so I lower my tone. "Okay, have you looked into all her friends? Maybe you missed one," I say. I hope he's getting the clue I am trying so hard to give him. I walk away, heading towards my car with purpose. I stare straight ahead and walk through the closest exit and I keep walking until I am safely inside my vehicle, then drive out of the complex. I hope Vi will forgive me for giving him a nudge.

If Orion takes the lead, this could be the moment that changes their lives for the better.

CHAPTER 6

Operation "Find the Fire"

Orion

What the fuck just happened? I just got my ass reamed out by the sweet little baker—that's what happened!

As I stand surrounded by my brothers and their wives, I am stunned into silence. Hanna knows much more than she is letting on. Why did Vi confide in her? Why not Maddie and Ava? Those three have been inseparable since meeting. Vi almost gave her life to save Maddie.

The longer I stand there, looking at her friends, the more it dawns on me. The women would be forced to keep secrets from their men. They would be put in an awkward position. The girls have been at an absolute loss over Vi's disappearance. They have relentlessly tried calling, without success. A sea of eyes are resting on me, waiting for me to say something.

I've tracked Vi's credit cards. She hasn't made a move on them. I checked hotels, motels, inns and other B&B accommodations from here to two states out on all sides. So, what am I missing?

"Orion."

I snap my head to Guard at the abruptness of my name being called to get my attention.

"We are waiting for the next move, man," he says. "What do you need from us?". I take in the vision of all my brothers, standing together, strong in their resolve, waiting for to me get clarity on my relationship with Vi. They watch silently, wondering if I am going to go back to the two very willing women, openly confessing to want to fuck me senseless, or fight to find the fire that lights my days and nights.

No contest!

My gaze rests on Risk. "I need to know everything there is to know about that spitfire little baker and her routine, Risk. She was giving me a very important piece of information and I think there is a lot she isn't saying. I don't know what I am going to find when I see Vi again, but I need to see this through," I tell him honestly.

"Yeah, and you owe her an apology when all is said and done. She handed you a gift and you were aggressive and laid your hands on her. That shit doesn't fly! Never with a woman and never in anger."

OPERATION "FIND THE FIRE"

Risk is pissed and very curt. His taunt jaw tells me he's holding back the urge to rip me a new one. This is an anomaly. Risk is typically a lot like me. Controlled.

"Once I get to the bottom of this and have time to set things straight with Vi, I will not only give her my sincerest apology, I will order every dessert known to man until the day I die," I reassure him. I see his lip curl upward and know that we are good.

"Great. Then we only have to figure out how to work off the extra sugar," he quipped, knowing full well he doesn't give a shit about that. "I'll get started on researching Hanna."

"Uh, Orion, I just remembered something. I mean it's probably nothing. I'm sure it's not important and may or may not have anything to do with Vi's disappearance," Ava says quietly. Guard protectively puts his arm around his wife, urging her to continue.

"What is it, baby?" he prods gently.

Ava looks befuddled but continues. "Well, I remember her having the flu or a cold or something for a long while. She kept cancelling our coffee dates," she says.

"That's right!" Maddie pipes in.

"Anyway, I suggested she see the doctor to get something for it since she couldn't seem to shake whatever virus she seemed to have," says Ava.

"I know she went because I offered to drive with her to keep her company, but she said she was fine to go alone and was feeling better that day. I called her that afternoon. She told me they gave her something and she would be good as new in a few weeks," Maddie recalls, tapping her foot. I can see that she is trying to reach into her memory for more details. She taps War's chest. "Dr. Riggs. That's the doctor she had an appointment with!" She beams with excitement.

"Good job, kitten," War growls lowly into her ear. Her smile spreads to light up her face, thrilled to be able to give us more information that will hopefully lead us to my missing woman.

War turns to me. "I got this angle. I'll find out what I can about the doc and the appointment. Risk takes the baker."

"Orion, you go back to her apartment. You may have missed something. Now that we know she left over some fucked-up decision to save you, we can focus on the where," Guard states, "My guess is that she is closer than we think and may be in hiding."

"Why do you say that?" I ask.

"Vi loves you. If there is even a hint of a chance to work things out, she's going to stick close," he says confidently. I sigh heavily and hope he's right.

"Operation, Find the Fire is underway!", exclaims Cris. He is the youngest recruit, soon to become a full member. He has stood strong with us. His bravery, intelligence and skills are a definite asset to our Pride. He is ever present, never backing down on a dark situation.

CHAPTER 7

The Shocking Debrief

Orion

It's been forty-eight hours since our operation dubbed "Find the Fire" first started. Cris thought it was appropriate given Vi's fiery spirit, matching hair, and personality. She would love the name. She would also tell us how to go about our investigation. She was a great little researcher, never left a stone unturned. Vi didn't give up and was a pit-bull when she was after information, and it almost cost her life. She kept digging into that fuckwad who was after Maddie. She knew too much and couldn't get out of the studio quick enough. The asshole took pleasure in giving Vi pain and beating her into unconsciousness. Maddie pulled the trigger to finally free Vi from his beating. I still shudder at the sight of seeing her bloody and broken.

The round table is surrounded by Pride Members. Guard calls the meeting to order.

"Risk, you're up," Guard announces.

"Right, well our resident shy baker girl was once married and is trying to get legally divorced. It's been five years and he has been stalling the legal proceedings at every opportunity. Hanna has asked that the divorce details be kept confidential. I am having someone work to gather more details about this asshole. For now, he continues to be a pain in the ass and contacts her every few months. The documents that I have uncovered show that the divorce was started after he pushed her down a flight of stairs. She cited physical and verbal abuse while intoxicated. She left town as soon as she filed and started over here in our town. She spends most of her time in the bakery. A few friends come around and ask her out, to which she rarely goes. No one has a bad thing to say about her, except her ex and his family. He's led them to believe that she is a gold digger, however while married, she was the only one employed, with two jobs. She was a bookkeeper and baked on weekend for special events. The mechanic shop she did bookkeeping for was really upset that she left. The owner tried to get her to stay and offered her protection, but she refused, stating that she didn't want anyone else to get hurt."

He takes breath and continues, "She has two sisters and a brother. Six nieces and nephews between them all. The men in her family, brothers and brothers-in-law, are fiercely protective of her. Every time she needs to go in front of the judge to move forward on the divorce, they all go with her. She purchased the family home, which is only a half hour from here. Her

THE SHOCKING DEBRIEF

family lives in that town. They are all close. She dotes on her nieces and nephews. She remembers every birthday and always makes a special, themed cake for every special occasion. I haven't been able to drive by and see her home outside of town or talk with the neighbors yet." He finishes and places the documents he gathered directly in front of me, so I can take a closer look.

I start to leaf through the information when I hear War's voice. "Well, I have been looking into Dr. Riggs, full name Dr. Madison Riggs. She has an impeccable reputation and has been a member of the hospital board of directors. She specializes in gynecology. She donates time to several non-profit organizations. She prides her practice on patient confidentiality and has agreements in place with all the nurses and staff who work in her practice. Despite her highly effective computer system, we were able to hack into Vi's file. Vi went in for flu like symptoms and her blood levels seemed off. They did tests and forwarded her results to another doctor by the name of Dr. Anne Radison." War stops talking, forcing me to look up from the paperwork I was reviewing. He is hesitating far too long. Fear grips me. Vi may be really sick. The worst scenarios pop into my head. The worst diseases come to mind topped. Jesus, I can't stand the silence.

"What, brother? What is it?" I roar. I get up, ready to pull the papers out of his hands and read them myself when Guard pulls my arm back.

"Sit down, bud. It's alright," he says smoothly. "It's not terminal, but it is a lifetime change."

I scan the room. Some have smirks. Many are looking down at their feet.

"Is someone going to give me this life-altering news, or do I have to beat it of you?" I snap. Risk sits down next to me.

"Brother, we got your back. We know that you have been through fire and have resurrected yourself here with Guard and Satan's Pride. This information should be coming from Vi and we think she should be the one to tell you. We haven't found her yet, and we think the reason she left is because you don't want to hear what she has to say. So, I am going to tell you and you can decide if Vi is worth finding." Risk nods at me waiting for me to acknowledge. I accept.

I view the table and see each member nod their head in agreement, Guard leading the pact, followed by War, Demon and ending with Cris.

"Let me have it." I steel my gaze to Risk and wait.

"Vi is pregnant with your baby," Risk declares firmly.

I stare blankly ahead at the grey wall, letting this sink into my brain. Memories of Lisa and the baby I couldn't protect flash into my mind. I wasn't there to protect them when they needed me the most. I was off defending my country and left my family unprotected. How am I going to be able to protect Vi and a baby now?

My baby.

"Everyone out," Guard orders. Feet shuffling, chairs scraping the floor, and then the slam of the door draw my eyes upward to Guard. He lowers himself into the chair next to me.

"I can't be a father," I whisper. "I can't keep them safe from the deviants who infiltrate our lives. I'm not sure I can even be the father I want to be. You know, Guard. You know my father was an asshole." My tone deepens, "What if I'm like him?" I ask. My mouth is dry, and I feel like vomiting.

"First, I see you with my son. I would put my child in your hands any day. If I ever thought my kid needed safeguarding, you would be my first choice. You are amazing with my boy. He loves you unconditionally and you aren't his father. But you are the best uncle he could ever ask for. You and the other brothers protect him when I am not around because I'm tending to club business. Your child will have an army at their back too. Our kids will have each other. They will grow together and learn how to protect one another. What happened to Lisa was not your fault. You cannot take responsibility for her being there that day or you not being there. You, risking your life for your country was a noble thing and do not make light of the sacrifices you made each and every day with your life. What happened was tragic, but it was not because you weren't there to protect them. Right here and now, you have the ability to give Vi all she needs. Your brothers will take your back whenever you need us. Vi and that baby will be cared for just like Ava and Gavin are. Just like Maddie. The question is, do you love Vi and do you want this child enough to officially make them part of our Pride family? Are you willing to make her part of your life and ours forever? Is she your one? Once you know the answer to that, we can move forward." Guard ends with a hand clamped on my shoulder.

I take a breath and then another. I faced him straight on. "I love her. I thought she knew. I was trying to hide her away from the crazy that seeps into our lives. Trying to keep her safe," I explain.

"Orion, it is not lost on any of us how you reacted to what happened with Vi and Maddie's stalker. We know that you are torn between losing her forever and keeping her hidden away. You took the brunt of the responsibility over what happened there. Truth is, we all fell short that day and we each feel responsible for not keeping her away from the studio. I promise you that that will never happen again. Cris is still beating himself up over her leaving the café without his knowledge," he continues, "Vi has been feeling you drift away from her. *She felt it*," he stresses. "Hell, we felt it. We are your family, so we thought we should give you time to grieve and reconnect. Vi didn't have that luxury when she found out she was pregnant."

I nod, knowing that Guard is right. I have been distant. I was putting space between us for fear that Vi would realize I wasn't enough to care for her. I have been a selfish prick. Worrying about how I feel; what I need. Fuck I am an asshole and not good enough for the greatness that makes all that is Vi. But I can't let her go because every moment I spent with her was pure heaven—until I royally screwed things up.

Now she is out there alone, pregnant with my baby, thinking that I don't give a fuck. Scared and lonely. I have to go get my girl.

"I have to find her, Prez," I choke out. "I want my woman; I want my baby. I want it all. Hopefully, Vi will still want me. If she doesn't, I don't want her hiding from anything," I tell him.

A heavy sigh escapes Guard. "Right. Let's go find your woman," he agrees. "I suggest a drive to

Hanna's family property. Also, I have to say this, and know it comes with the deepest of love for you, man, you've spent so long keeping her out of your emotional life that you missed all that makes Vi, *Vi*. You may not know who she is completely, and I suggest you take the time to see what you missed."

"I love her, Guard. Whatever I missed I'm going to learn, and we will get through it all. The good and the bad," I vow.

CHAPTER 8

Meeting of the Minds

Vi

Thousands of colourful beads sit in perfectly aligned containers, all labelled and strewn out over the fold-away table I found in the garage. I threw a lavender with black trim shawl overtop of it, making it homier and less utilitarian. I didn't need to pack very much when I let Molly's. My apartment was furnished. I ate most of my meals at Molly's or the Club. All I really had to pack were my clothes, books, CDs, and knickknacks that I had accumulated over the last few years. Most were trinkets and gifts from Orion. I couldn't bear to leave them behind. They were both a beautiful and tormenting reminder of our time together.

I'm not sure how I can feel so nostalgic and sad to the point of tears whenever I reach out and touch a simple scarf. He bought it one night when we were walking. I shivered when the temperature dropped that evening and Orion immediately slipped into the closest shop and purchased a bright red scarf with hues of grey throughout. I feel a tear slide down my cheek as I recall that evening, running the material through my fingers. Orion gently wrapped the warm material around my throat, then pulled me close to kiss my nose. "Never goin' to let the cold in. I'll keep you warm," he whispered against my lips. And tears continued to fall. He is a grizzly of a man, but with me, he was my gentle giant.

A loud knock on the door pulls me out of my melancholy stupor. I wipe away the tears and head to the door. It's probably Hanna. She is always dropping by or calling to make sure I am doing well. I think my mini meltdown has pulled us closer. Hanna has been asking me persistently to call Orion. She may be right, and he does have the right to know that he is a father. I fully believe that he will want to "make it right". He will want me to come back and take care of me and the baby. But I don't want him to "do the right thing" out of obligation.

I could live with almost being loved, my baby however, deserves it all. Two parents to spoil, teach, and love our little peanut. Unfortunately, my baby will have to make do with just me. I will do all I can to make sure he or she has all their needs met.

The knock is louder and more persistent now. I race over to the door and throw it open.

I stop cold, feeling the blood drain from my face as I find before me, a massive chest. I know that chest. I lift my eyes to encounter that come-hither smile. I peruse those luscious lips and sensual mouth. He looks just as sexy as he always does except his eyes seems distraught and tired.

I take a step back, allowing the door to swing open even wider, giving way to allow Orion to walk straight into the hall. I gawk. I have no words. It's been over a month and until now, he hasn't come to find me and as far as I know hasn't even looked. I thought he had moved on.

He looks me over from top to toe. His eyes finally settle on mine, then once again looks me up and down. I clutch my belly, consciously trying to cover my bump. I am hoping that my rounded tummy isn't too noticeable.

"You've lost weight, baby. We're going to have to do something about that," he growls.

I snap out of it and tap into my inner badass. "To what do I owe the pleasure, Orion?" I say snidely.

He continues to walk through my home, taking it all in, taking note of my table filled with pretty baubles. I have a soft caramel throw that used to lay over the end of my bed at Molly's, now over the footrest in the family room. He scans the room, fixating on the shawl I was holding just moments ago. He reaches out and holds it firmly in his grip as he plops himself down on the sofa. Which looks extremely small with him on it.

I take a breath. I can't give in to the hope that he has come for me. He probably wants closure. Okay, I can do this. I can give him the closure he needs to move on.

"Come sit, Vi," he commands like I am going to roll over on demand.

Well, now I am peeved. Orion walks into my home, makes himself comfortable on *my* couch and then tells me to come to him like a lapdog. Nah uh, that shit doesn't sit well with me. I slam the door with force and stalk over to Orion, standing directly in front of him, hands on hips, bending at the waist until I am in his personal space.

"Listen, Orion, if you are here to end things, then go about having your say and get out. But do not think you can waltz in here and bark orders at me like I am some pitiful puppy awaiting your attention," I say, my chest heaving with fury. I am holding back to stop myself from physically slapping the smirk off his face.

I recognize that look. I can see that he is trying to get a rise out of me. I calm my breathing and close my eyes to regain composure. I am suddenly dragged onto the sofa beside him, his hands holding me steady to stop me from bolting back up. He knows me far too well.

"Look into my eyes, Vi," he says quietly. I shake my head, refusing to make contact with those eyes. I will crumble if I make contact.

"Please, pretty girl, I need you to see me when I say what I have to say," he pleads as he gives my hand a squeeze. He hasn't called me pretty girl since the hospital. Those words work through my core. He's never called me that when we were with anyone else, but alone, and especially in bed, he would whisper pretty girl in my ear.

With superhuman strength I would never have believed I was capable of, I lifted my chin and meet his gaze.

"Vi, my pretty girl, I have been selfish. I held myself back and although I have a dozen reasons for why I did, it doesn't excuse that I was a bastard for making you feel that you didn't matter. I took from you. Everything you gave, I took. You offered, and I took, thinking that I was giving you enough. But enough isn't good enough. You deserve it all. I need you to come home with me and let me make this right. I want to explore what we have. If what we had in the past was really good, then what we will have will be spectacular," he says emphatically.

He wants me to come home with him. My heart leaps for joy and then suddenly plummets. I need to tell him now before he commits too much of himself. I want to cry.

"I don't know what to say," I tell him. "Why now? We've been together over two years and you made it clear that you were perfectly satisfied with how things were. The last six months, you have closed yourself off and let me down. You have been holding me at arm's length and it was getting worse each and every time we were together." I pull in a shuddered breath on the verge of new tears. "That hurt me." My voice cracks. "It hurt so much." I sob.

"There is so much I haven't said, Vi. And before you say anything, you're right, I should have said it all months ago. Baby, you leaving like you did almost buried me. I went insane looking for you and when I couldn't find you, I became a bigger asshole. I know I have a lot to make up for. You are my first priority. Then I need to make it up to my brothers," he shares.

"Before this goes any further, I need to tell you something," I say warily. I hesitate. He may get up and walk right out the door. I'm so scared. My lower lip trembles.

"Just say it, pretty girl. Whatever it is, we will figure it out," he says in a steely tone.

I blurt out, "I'm pregnant," then shut my eyes tight. I don't want to see the anger in his face. I ready myself in case he decides to walk out the door.

"I want those pretty eyes, baby," he teases, "I've missed them for too long."

I blink to see him grinning. "I hope my little girl has eyes just like her mommy," he says quietly.

I burst into tears. Damn hormones. He holds me close, maneuvering me in his arms and manages to place me lightly in his lap. The pent-up emotions open to a flood of happy tears.

"It might be a boy," I tease, trying to ease the onslaught of information into a more light-hearted atmosphere.

"Don't care, pretty girl. As long as you are both healthy, I'm good. I can deal with whatever comes my way," Orion says with determination in his tone.

"I hesitate to say this with this moment being so wonderful," I begin, but am cut off by Orion.

"Tell me. No fear, Vi," he pushes.

"Suffice to say there is a lot we haven't shared and if this is going to work between us, we are going to have to have a meeting of the minds," I tell him softly, caressing his beard and stoking his cheek.

"I know we have to talk, and we need to figure out where we wanna go and how we plan to get there. But for the next hour, I want to hold you and enjoy this moment. Just me and my pretty girl," he says as he cinches my waist and places a firm hand on my belly. "I didn't think I would ever see your beauty again," he confesses.

Our hearts are speaking to one another, even if we haven't vocalized all of our thoughts yet. Our meeting of the minds has turned into the meeting of our hearts and souls.

CHAPTER 9

Diamond not Teflon

Orion

She is in my arms and everything is right in the world; at least for now. There are many discussions to be had and decisions to be made, but in this moment, I don't want to overwhelm Vi all at once.

Vi has lost weight. She is frail; I can see the bones of her collarbone. This doesn't detract from her beauty; however, it guts me that she has been going through all these changes alone and once again, I was self-absorbed. All that changes right the fuck now!

I convince Vi she should go and lay down for a while after she vaulted off my lap and ran for the bathroom. I was too stunned to move until I heard her become violently ill.

I raced into the small bathroom and watched her wretch into the toilet, holding back her hair and stroking her back. Vi eventually sagged on her haunches and tried to push herself up. I lifted her slowly and placed her gently on the counter. I took a cool cloth and placed it on the back of her neck, then helped her brush her teeth and wipe her face. She began to protest that she could do it herself to which I replied, "You've been doing this alone for too long. Let me take care of you, pretty girl."

She relented immediately. A small smile appeared on her pale lips. I took her into the tiny bedroom she claimed as her own, refusing to take the larger master bedroom offered by Hanna. I lay her down cautiously, and sank in beside her, unwilling to let her out of my arms just yet. I stroked her hair and her eyes eventually drifted shut. I listened to her breath even out and stayed until I was sure she was asleep. I covered her with the blanket from the bottom of the bed forcing myself to not look back. I knew that I would be tempted to climb back into bed with her and have the world around us disappear. But I needed to make some calls.

Here I am, pulling the phone out of my pocket and hitting the too tiny buttons with my massive fingers to connect to Guard.

"What do you need, brother?" I hear on the other end. No recriminations, no lecture. My brothers rally to give me and my Vi whatever we may need. No questions asked.

"I need a real estate agent to find my family a home. I need an appointment with Vi's doctor because she is losing weight fast and I can't remember Ava ever looking like that during her pregnancy; like Vi looks right now. But most of all, my woman needs her girls to rally and give her some love. As much as I hate to share her, her needs are more important than mine," I say gruffly.

"Real estate agent, I'll get War on that. Make a list of the must haves and we will make it happen. Doctor, I'll get Risk to make that appointment for Monday. He can be very persuasive. That'll give her a couple of days with her girls pampering her." In the background, Maddie and Ava are being chirpy and asking a shit ton of questions like Where is she? and Can we go see her now?

"Not sure if you can hear our Lady Pride but they have been next to impossible to keep down waiting for the opportunity to see Vi. I had to keep Ava busy with creative sex," I hear Guard tease.

"I can't believe you told him that!" I hear Ava huff. "See if you get any tonight."

"Baby, you're addicted to me like I'm addicted to you," he volleys.

"Prez, as entertaining as this is, I need to get back to VI," I say. "You can come by this afternoon. Bring food if you can. I don't want to leave her right now to grab groceries and don't want her cooking." I lower my voice to continue, "I'm worried Guard. She is fucking pale and not gaining weight. I expected to see her fuller but the only thing that stands out is a baby belly. And that's not much." This can't be healthy for her or the baby.

"No worries, man. We will get there for one o'clock and will get a plan in place to get our Vi back to healthy. We will come food in hand. We got your back, Orion, just like you've had ours for the last ten years." The confidence in his tone gives me a sense of relief.

I hang up the phone, tossing it on the kitchen table and take the time to finally take in my surroundings. The house is small, neat and tidy and definitely looks like a woman lives in it. There's a light pink and cream white sofa with tons of pillows thrown over it and I recognize the wraps and scarves that belong to Vi.

Vi was making this her home. Adding her personal touches to make it her place. I saunter into the kitchen to find lemon squares. Hanna's contribution to keeping Vi comfortable. The fridge is fully stocked with fresh fruits and vegetables and a note plastered to the front with a magnet that reads:

Place what you need on the list. I will be happy to pick it up when I come back.
Hugs,
Hanna

Hanna has been Vi's fairy godmother. Taking care of her, making sure she has groceries in the refrigerator. She gave Vi her home to live in. Watches out for her and got my head out of my ass and led me back to her. I will make this right with Hanna. An apology isn't going to be enough. I always pay my debts as Vi is priceless, as is our baby. Hanna has just found herself an ally.

I trudge through the rest of the place and notice the table with beads, strings, soldering tools, and what look like earrings and other jewelry strewn all over it.

A computer in the corner of the room has a picture on it. As I move closer, I see a prototype for a business card. *Vi-vacious Designs.* I am stunned. She makes jewelry? When did this start?

I start looking more closely. My gaze fixes on a ball of yarn and knitting needles with a pattern on how to knit a baby blanket. She knits too?

I grasp the yarn in my hand and sit myself down on the sofa. I breathe deep. I made it so she felt she could never be all that she is with me. I held back, so she held back. I am a goddamned fucking idiot!

My girl, she is made of Teflon and I took from her and she stood strong. She followed her own path alone and never asked me for a damn thing. She ran to protect our baby because she thought I couldn't love them. Teflon.

"Is everything okay?" Vi's voice is sleepy until she notices the wool I am caressing between my fingers.

My eyes meet hers. "Everything is perfect, baby," I say loud and strong.

My Vi. Not Teflon—she is my diamond. Stronger and more beautiful than any gem.

CHAPTER 10

Lady Pride Members take a stand

Orion

Vi makes coffee as we get caught up on all we missed over the last couple of months. I tell her all about the brothers searching for her. I confess about my almost grave mistake that Hanna had the good sense to yell at me about. I contemplate telling her about Lisa, but I just can't bring myself to go down that road. Not yet, anyway, but I will. I am not sure that she can handle any more in her condition.

Vi explains her reasons for leaving. She recounts the visit to the doctor and how she was sure it was simply a stubborn flu bug. Vi tears when she talks about not knowing whether to jump for joy or fall apart. Since I had become more compartmentalized, she thought this was the only option she had left. She understood she was making the only logical choice. Especially for me. I wanted to know if she ever considered not having my baby. Her response was, "This is the best part of you and me. He or she is absolutely perfect, and I haven't even met them. I can't let our baby go."

Pretty girl tells me about her dreams to design jewelry and clothes, focusing on one-of-a-kind designs. Then she tells me about the shops that are carrying her product and how excited she is to try and make this a viable full-time business. She currently has a dozen or so shops on her roster and is hoping to attract more with her website. The necklaces and bracelets have been her best sellers however the new accessories she has added to the collections are becoming more popular. The glint in her eyes when she talks about the belts, buckles, and hair clips make her totally fuckable.

"And you knit," I declare as I point to the yarn in the box beside the sofa.

"Yeah," she says shyly. "That's new. I wanted something to calm me. I tried it and found it soothing. I really enjoy it." She beams. "Maybe eventually I'll add knits and crochet tops to the Website."

I have never seen Vi this relaxed and happy. Truly happy. She pours our coffee and is about to take her first sip when I ask, "Pretty girl, should you be drinking coffee? Won't it hurt the baby?"

Vi giggles. "I can have one a day of regular coffee and decaf beyond that, if I want it. It's the only

LADY PRIDE MEMBERS TAKE A STAND

thing I crave and in all honesty it's the only thing that helps me get the toast down. I haven't had much of an appetite and when I do get something down, it unsettles my stomach and makes its way back up," she replies somberly.

I make my way over to her and place my hands on either side, trapping her against the counter with my large frame, boxing her in. "I'm worried, baby. You've lost weight, quite a bit of it and I just witnessed how violently ill you were just an hour ago."

"I'll be fine. I have another appointment in three weeks with the doctor and I will tell her about still not being able to keep my meals down. Plus, I am scheduled to do bloodwork, urine, and the whole she-bang. I remember her talking about checking weight, diet, and all that," she says, then places her hands on either side of my face. "We'll be alright, baby." She kisses my mouth sweetly. I pull her closer and lean more deeply into her. Taking my time to lick and nip her lower lip. Vi melts into me. I haven't tasted this sweetness for a long time, and it is intoxicating. I press my body firmly against hers until we are connected from chest to thighs. Her arms wrap around my neck. My head is saying that we need to take it slow, she has been ill and needs tenderness. My cock is saying lay her on the floor and pound into her. A nagging chiming of the doorbell pulls us both reluctantly out of our embrace.

Our lips are a whisper apart. "They'll come back," she says breathlessly.

"Doubt that, sugar. Ava and Maddie won't be deterred. Those women are dogs with a bone when they get something in their sights."

Her face softens. I know she wants to see her girls and she was pleased that I called for them to visit.

"Yep," she says and pulls away to answer the door. I hang back; I am going to need another minute to adjust my crotch and settle down before seeing them.

"Let the healing begin!" Ava shouts loud and boisterously, as she plows through the door with a giggling Gavin on her hip.

"Don't you ever leave us again. You are the original member of our Lady Pride, and shall I remind you of the oath we all made to one another that we will always be there for each other, no matter what comes." Ava's tiny body shakes with passion then she pulls Vi in for a hug, holding tight to her best friend, while baby Gavin pats Vi's face. Maddie joins Ava and Vi with tears streaming down her face as they hold each other close.

Vi has her family and I have her.

"Kitten, move your lovefest into the other room," I hear War tell the ladies. "We are bringing in food and need a clear path to the kitchen."

"Be good, honey," Maddie soothes.

"Kitten, I am always good. You should know. You were with me all night." He winks as he passes the reunion to dump a box on the kitchen table, followed by Guard and the others.

I hear a car engine outside the house and look out to see who it is. Hanna is sitting inside her SUV, watching the line of motorcycles lining the driveway. I see her hesitate and know that she is about to take off again.

"I'll be right back," I say to War and run out before she takes off. I knock on the driver's side door and a startled Hanna squeaks in surprise, then proceeds to lower the window.

"Why don't you come inside and celebrate with us?" I ask.

"Oh no," she says, "I should get back and get a head start with the orders I have due tomorrow" I can see her admiring the closeness of the three women. A brief flicker of sadness crosses her face.

"They would want you in there," I tell her. "I want you here with us as well. Without you, this wouldn't have happened," I admit.

"You would have found your way back to each other." Hanna smiles slyly. "I just think that neither of you needed to continue suffering any more than necessary."

I smile back, "I don't know what you need, but whatever it is, whenever you need me, you call me." I give her my promise, my marker. "My word is my honor."

"Thank you, Orion. I just need you to remember how it felt without her. Please don't mess this up. She adores you," Hanna states. "I'll be going now. I hope to see you both at the bakery soon. Vi loves her lemon squares."

I release the handle of the door and step back. I can see that I won't be able to convince her to come in and join the reunion. This woman just bought an army at her back whenever she needs us.

CHAPTER 11

Give and take

Vi

I watch Ava with baby Gavin in her arms. Swinging him about and having Guard take him and fly him around the room. His baby giggle is adorable and contagious. Immediately I feel the pull to have a little boy with Orion's wild, unruly hair, mischievous eyes that crinkle slightly when he smiles and are piercingly serious when he is angry. I pat my belly and caress my little babe.

"I missed you, Vi," Maddie interjects my thoughts, holding out a glass of cranberry juice, while taking a sip of her drink.

"I missed you too, Maddie," I say and I truly have missed my girls. I also think of how fortunate I am to have had Hanna to lean on during this time.

ORION

"We were really worried. I didn't know what to do. Ava was a mess and burst into tears each time I mentioned your name. War and Guard were exhausted dealing with our emotional outbursts and organizing searches to find you," she chastises. "I was so very afraid for you, Vi." She sniffles as I watch a single tear run down her cheek.

I hold her hand, taking in the severity of the pain I have caused my dearest friends and pangs of guilt fill my heart. I recall the emotional texts and fearful messages; I begin to sob with her.

"I never wanted that for you and Ava or anyone." I hiccup. "I thought you would move on and forget me once Orion moved on," I whisper.

"Orion was a basket case. At first, he was worried sick and tore the town apart looking for you. He had feelers out in multiple states. Then he started drinking heavily and it was really bad Vi. He finally got out of his drunken stupor when Hanna let him have it. He was being so stupid that I wanted to smack him silly," she says. "I told War there was something wrong and War insisted that we stay out of it. We got into a horrible fight about it because I was on my way to see Orion and War lost his mind. Needless to say, he stopped me," she finished.

I am stunned that she would go to such lengths. I never thought that they would go to so much trouble for me. No one has ever looked out for me before. I have left other towns and never has anyone come after me.

"Damn," I say. "I am so very sorry that you and War were fighting over me and Orion. Truly, it was never my intention." We have caused so much trouble for our friends.

"We know, Vi. Ava and I know that you would never do anything to hurt us. Especially me, Vi," she continues, "I know the sacrifice you made to keep me safe. I was there when you refused to tell him where I was and took the beating that was meant for me. I think that's why I got so mad at Orion. He wasn't right. What he did just wasn't right. He was there but he wasn't *there*. We all tried to get him to talk it out, but he wouldn't. I still don't know why," she says, still confused by Orion's actions. "I do know that Guard and Risk know more than anyone else about his story and they are not talking. Risk says that it is his story to tell and we have to respect that." Maddie touches my belly. "I am so excited for a new baby. War and I have started talking about a baby as well. War thinks it's best that I complete my touring commitments first and I agree. I am also a little selfish and want a little more one-on-one time with War before we add another little Pride baby to the mix." She laughs.

I laugh too. "I am still sorry that I was the cause of your argument."

"No worries," she blushes, flicking her wrist to indicate that it was nothing. "Make up sex is awesome," she adds, making me laugh harder and louder than I have in months.

"Food's up, ladies," Risk bellows from the other room.

We make our way over to the barrage of dishes splayed across the counter and tables. Many of the guys have already made plates for themselves and are strewn about the house on any available chairs, sofas and even on the floor. Orion reaches out to take my hand as I approach. He leads me toward the cornucopia of aromas and as I approach, my stomach revolts in disgust. I yank out of his hold and cover my mouth as I run to the bedroom and sit on the edge of the bed forcing myself to take in deep, steady breaths. My eyes were so excited at the sight of the delicious array of food; however, my stomach is saying definitely not. Orion rushes in on my tail and kneels down in front of me.

"Vi, are you alright?" he asks with great concern in his tone.

I nod, not trusting my voice yet.

"Babe, this can't go on. You have not eaten a single thing since I got here and I gotta say, it looks like you've lost far too much weight for a woman who should be eating for two," Orion declares. His concern is touching.

I see he is frowning, and his brow is furrowed. Orion places his hands on my thighs and gently caresses them. "I want to eat; I truly do. Then the smells are too strong and I can't seem to get anything down without gagging," I tell him.

"Okay, pretty girl, you wait here," he commands as he gets up off his haunches and exits the room with purpose.

He walks in a few minutes later with a plate with a single plain bagel, lightly toasted with a smidgen of butter. He aligns himself to sit behind me with his legs splayed out on either side of mine. He lifts one half of the bagel to my lips. "Take a small bite, baby."

I take a nibble and chew slowly. I am cautious about whether I will need to jump up and find the toilet. Orion waits patiently until I swallow before lifting it again to my mouth. It takes what seems like forever but in real time about hour before I finish it all.

GIVE AND TAKE

I take small sips of the herbal tea that Ava brought in while Orion was feeding me. This is the most I have eaten in one sitting in weeks.

"Babe, we have an appointment on Monday with the doctor. We need to find out if you and the baby are doing okay," he tells me.

I blink. We have reconnected for less than a day and already he is making decisions on my behalf. I am enraged. "You made an appointment with the doctor without consulting me?" I say in a menacing tone.

"You haven't been well, Vi. I want ensure that you are both well," he responds.

"I recall mentioning that I already have an appointment to see my doctor in three weeks," I remind him.

"Three weeks is a long way off with you puking your guts out three to four times a day. You can barely stand. You are always tired and the weight you've lost scares the hell out of me," he bellows, raising his voice and dictating as if I don't have a say.

Then it hits me. He is worried about the baby not getting the nourishment it needs. Maybe that's why he wants to be here. It has nothing to do with me. Orion has a strong sense of honor and he may be doing this out of obligation.

"Did you know about the baby before you came here to see me?" I ask looking him directly in the eyes. His jaw clenches and his eyes shut tight. I know my answer. "You knew." I scramble off the bed to put some space between us. Orion reaches out to grab my hand. I jerk out of his grasp.

"It's not me you came for, it's the baby," I spew with indignation. "I am an unwanted add on."

"Have you lost your mind?" Orion roars and storms out the door, slamming it hard. I hear voices in the other room.

"Where are you going?" Guard asks.

"To get some air," spews Orion.

"Not alone you aren't. War ride with him," he commands, followed by the front door slamming.

I crawl back into bed and grab the cover and yank it up to my chest. I regret my words immediately. I could have asked instead of accusing him. However, what right does he have to rearrange my appointments and take over my life.

"Guard, let me talk to her," I hear Ava say.

"No. I have watched my club be ripped apart on several occasions and this one bit of insanity stops here and now," Guard exclaims.

Two thunderous legs plod into my room and view my grief-stricken face. His features soften as he pulls up a chair to sit by my bed.

"Vi, I have all the love in my heart for you. Not just because you are Ava's girl and made her feel wanted the minute she got here. Not because of the way you put your life on the line for Maddie. I love you like my little sister. I can understand that your head might be a little muddled. You think Orion is here for the wrong reasons and I am here to tell you that what you are thinking is utter bullshit. I have been a personal witness to that man tearing town after town apart looking for you. Endless hours of monitoring computer data in the hopes of getting a hit so he would have a place to start looking," Guard says firmly.

"I don't know why I said that," I tell him honestly. My hands clasp together in my lap, feeling like a stupid schoolgirl who was sent to the principal's office.

"I do," he says. I stare at him blankly. "Vi, he knows he fucked up. He knows that he should have been more open with you. He is also trying to make it right." He pauses. "Vi, I have seen the beauty of what the two of you have. I have also been witness to Orion fucking up and pulling away and not giving you the full understanding of why." Then he takes my hand, "And with the greatest of love, I say this—you let him Vi. You didn't push for an answer. You let him live in his head and you never gave him the opportunity to tell you how he feels about this baby. It seems to me Vi that you need to take some responsibility as well."

"Oh Guard, I screwed up. What am I going to do?" I cry. Guard is right. Totally and completely correct. I was too afraid to make him talk to me.

"He'll be back, Vi. He just needs to take a step back and breathe it out. This has all been happening really fast and he is working too hard at getting it right," he says. "In the meantime, come out, talk to your friends and be here when he gets back so that he knows you're okay."

I go the bathroom to wash my face. I pull myself together and decide that Guard is very well-informed on all that is Orion which means I should follow his lead.

Everyone has had their fill of food and we're doing clean up when I walked into the kitchen. I grab a fresh plate, piling on all of Orion's favorites. I am sure that he was too busy looking after me to get anything for himself. The front door opens as I am wrapping his plate. I stare at Orion in the doorway. My lips tremble and I race to meet him. Launching myself into his arms, I wrap my legs around his waist and bury my face in his neck. "I am so sorry," I cry.

"Shh, pretty girl. I am too," he replies gruffly. "I think we need to play a little game called give and take, Vi. I need to say so much and I am not sure where to start. I think you do too."

He walks me over to the armchair and plants himself into it with me still holding on strong. I lift my head to face him. "Give and take?" I ask.

"Yea, I give you a piece of me and you take the time to process. You feel free to share all that is you as well, Vi. I want to know all of you. I thought I did and now I know that you are even more complicated than I imagined," he teases.

"I'm not complicated. I was going for mysterious," I tease back.

Ava brings over the plate of food I set aside for Orion and we sit together with our friends until it's time for everyone to go. It is an amazing afternoon after all the drama. Orion is attentive, with his arm around me, kissing my neck and caressing my cheek.

CHAPTER 12

Soft and slow

Orion

We spent the afternoon with family. My brothers and their old ladies, with the added benefit of little Gavin. Gavin started in Ava's arms, then he wriggled his body over to Maddie, who sang to him until his droopy eyes finally fell shut. Guard took him into the bedroom, murmuring quietly as he nestled into the pillows.

This is the only family of mine that I have ever shared with Vi. It'll soon be time to tell her about my biological family too.

I don't even know how to begin. I have a biological brother. Nathan is an engineer, working for dear old dad in his business. Just how dad wanted it. Nathan is a good guy, but we only see each other when we can, which isn't easy since I've been disowned by my parents and Nate's future is in running the company. His world consists of his wife, Emily, and hopefully two point five kids in the next three to five years before taking over for Dad. Nate and I get together when he is in town to have a drink or have dinner and each time he tries to convince me that I should apologize to our dad and come home to help him run the company and take over the IT department.

He expects me to apologize for taking off to serve my country. Apologize for marrying a woman he didn't choose. Apologize for falling apart, for joining a brotherhood that didn't judge me, for being the man I choose to be instead of his heir in business. Mom would be so pissed at the separation. Angela Moore would have sat us all down and made us come to mutual decision, as she would put it. Instead she died of breast cancer, in pain and without Dad present. Another reason why Ian Moore is simply unimportant to me. Nate, I give my time to, because he makes an effort and I believe that we have a common bond, not of blood but of understanding that we both lived with the loss of Mom and the dictatorship of Dad. So here I am, Gavin Deacon Moore, IT and Special Ops expert with a brotherhood of the heart instead of blood, to share that Vi and I are having a baby and celebrating.

I'll call Nate tomorrow and let him know. He will make a special trip to meet Vi. This means I need to tell Vi. Tomorrow is going to be a long day.

As the last man is leaving, I tell Vi to go get ready for bed, giving me time to recover from having her on my lap, touching her and kissing her neck. Breathing in her scent of vanilla and watching her laugh whole heartedly for the first time in fuckin' months. The minute she jumped into my arms after having gone for a ride with War to settle myself down, I knew I wasn't letting her go, so I settled her on my lap and that's where she stayed for the better part of the evening.

As I lock the house down, I notice a car across the street. The engine revs then takes off. I don't know this area and I for damn sure don't know the neighbours but I can feel the hair on my neck stand on end and this makes me wary. I gotta get Vi into our own home, so that is going to be priority two, right after the appointment with the doctor.

I saunter to the bedroom and stop dead when I see Vi in my tee, with the sheets pulled up to her waist. It's always been her favorite and she wore it to bed every night she stayed over. I teased her all the time about wanting to wear it one day only to have found it missing and sitting in her drawer. She would always say, "It smells like you so when you leave our bed, I still have you with me." Even then she was telling me I was enough.

"You're wearing my tee," I tell her. She smiles with a broad grin.

"Yup," she answers, stilling smiling huge. "I saw it on the top of your bag. You brought it for me," she said softly. "Thank you. I missed it and I missed you."

I walk over and place my fists in the bed, making an indentation on either side of Vi's legs. "Missed you too, pretty girl. I love you, Vi. And hear me, I love you for all that you are and all that you are going to share with me that I don't know yet. I love our baby because they're ours," I tell her, looking into her eyes, making sure she feels what I feel in this moment—completed. "Never letting you go, baby."

With that, she places her arms around my neck and presses her lips to mine. I immediately take over, feeling the softness of her lip, and dipping my tongue between her lips, deepening our kiss until we are both gasping for air. "Jesus Christ, baby, you keep this up, I am going to need to go out for another ride to cool off."

She lifts herself onto her knees and moves her hands under my Henley and lifts it up and over my head before tossing it to the floor.

"Vi," I warn.

"I want to feel you close, my grizzly," she says then proceeds to kiss my chest with soft butterfly kisses.

She makes a move to unzip my pants, when I stop her by closing my hand over hers. I have got to put a stop to this. No way I am going to fuck Vi until I know that it's safe and she is well enough. I am never putting her in danger and that means even from me.

"Pretty girl, you have not been well. I want to make sure that all is good before we take the time to reacquaint my body with yours," I say teasingly.

"I ache for you, grizzly," she says. She calls me Grizzly when we are in bed together. Her voice is low and sexy as she whispers in my ear.

"Baby, we gotta take this soft and slow," I remind her.

My girl is running hot and it's my role to make sure my girl gets whatever she needs. I run my hands up her thighs to cup her ass. Her panties barely cover her firm bottom as I slide my fingers under them. So soft and smooth. I bend my head to nuzzle her neck.

"Alright, pretty girl, this is how it's goin' to go.

SOFT AND SLOW

You are going to remove my tee and lay back. I'm going to have my fun with this beautiful body and make sure you get what you need." I nip at her ear, which evokes a hoarse moan. "You with me, baby?"

"Yeah," she responds breathlessly.

"Do it, Vi. Nice and slow," I command. I take my hands away and Vi sways slightly to allow our touch to linger. She proceeds to remove the tee with deliberate hesitation, inching the hem up over her hips, above her belly, where my eyes stare for a moment, before following the path to her naked chest. I watch her toss the shirt away and gape at her luscious, full breasts.

Vi has always been beautiful. She has always eaten well and exercised and taken pride in being strong. She wanted to have a healthy body. Now, her breasts are fuller, and her belly is rounder. Thinner but still beautiful. Vi does as she's told and lays back.

I lay next to her, moving my fingers to remove the curl from her cheek and kiss her passionately. I love her taste. I can get drunk on the taste of Vi. She makes a move to touch me. "No, baby. Tonight is for you."

I revive my attack on her senses. I lick and place kisses along her collar bone, and progress down her body. I run my hands over her breasts, massaging and plucking the nipples gently. I watch her face; she pulls her lower lip between her teeth and allows a meaningful mewl. "Soft and slow, Vi," She lifts her breasts to move closer and I take a nipple into my mouth. Lavishing her bud with licks and tiny bites, moving on to suckle until she is squirming in delight. I move my attention to her twin and am enjoying the show as she contorts and pants. Lips full and pouting; I can't help myself and taste them again and again.

God, I love the sounds she's making. I follow the path down her stomach, taking care to caress her tenderly. I move my body between her legs and begin kissing her thighs to her knees. "Spread, pretty girl," I hum while continuing my assault and guide her legs apart, bending them at the knees before opening her wide. The sight of her pink pussy, glistening with need drives me wild.

"You don't—", Vi gasps and is quickly stopped when my tongue hits its target. The sound of her gasps and pants are making me even harder. I maneuver my hand and unlatch my belt, freeing my cock and I palm myself as I suck and lick at Vi's clit. I know she's close. Her hand reaches into my hair, not knowing whether to pull me closer or push me away because of the intensity of her oncoming orgasm. I am going to make her scream my name.

"Get there!" I command. "Say it, pretty girl!" She knows; she knows what I want to hear.

"Baby," she moans.

"Say it," I repeat.

"I... I... Oh!" she gasps. "My grizzly, oh my! My man, my grizzly!" she screams as her orgasm comes over her and she shudders her release. I continue to suck gently until she is calm. I am on my knees between her legs, still stroking my cock. She reaches and continues to stroke me, just how I like it. She knows me. I like it hard and I love the sight of her hands on me.

"Vi," I warn.

"Blow, baby. I wanna watch you come. I love looking at you when you come," she taunts. She bends to kiss the tip as she stokes. I come undone and let out my roar of gratification.

SOFT AND SLOW

I roll over onto my back beside her and before I have the opportunity to stop her, she is out of bed and has come back to clean me up, then races back into the bathroom where I hear the water running, then slides back into bed beside me.

I pull Vi closer to my side and tuck her in close. "Pretty girl, next time, you stay in bed and I clean us up."

"I wanted to," she says sleepily.

"Vi," I say.

"Orion, you take care of me and I want to take care of you." She lifts her eyes to mine. "I want to, and you need to let me."

I know where this is going. This is not just about this moment. Vi is saying that she has my back. Perfect for me. Tomorrow will come and I will have to let her in.

Soft and slow, and together. We'll get there.

CHAPTER 13

Pink Glitter

Vi

The room is filled with pregnant women and three huge men with Satan's Pride jackets squeezed in alongside them, looking completely uncomfortable. Well, two looking uncomfortable and one who has decided that waiting did not suit his schedule and is standing at the reception desk making it known.

"We have an appointment for nine o'clock," Orion states.

"I am aware sir; however, the doctor is currently in with a patient and is working as quickly as possible to get to you," the receptionist says to placate my grizzly bear.

"Vi has been sick for months and is not waiting

another minute. Get the doctor out here," he commands.

"Stop, Orion. They are doing their best," I say as I stand and place my hand through his arm to pull him back. A very agitated receptionist escapes to the back as I divert Orion's attention. "You are scaring these lovely ladies," I tell him.

He looks up and scans the room, noticing that most are looking at him like he's a dedicated daddy looking after his baby's mommy. Awe and reverence, not fear, but at least I got his attention diverted for a few minutes.

He turns back to me. "They are not." He tags my hand and leads me to a chair. "Sit down, Vi, I got this," he says.

"Vi, I am Josephine," a sweet melodic voice says from behind Orion. We both turn to see a lovely dark haired woman whose eyes appear to be a mix of blue and indigo.

"Hi," I greet her, and wave my hand toward Orion. "This is my guy, Orion.".

"Hey," is all Orion says with a chin lift in her direction.

"Would you like to follow me?" she asks, motioning us towards an empty room. Once there, Josephine says, "I thought that instead of waiting out there we could get you started on the ultrasound and the doctor can come in as soon as she is finished with her current patient. Is that alright?"

I nod happily. I have been dying to know what we are having. We had to wait until I was sixteen weeks in before I could make the appointment, then had to wait another week before I could get in. I tug on

Orion's hand and he looks down at me, "I want to know if it's a girl or a boy. Are you okay with that, or do you want a surprise?" I ask. I hope he wants to know. I have been dying to know that sex of the baby.

"I want to know. Need to see if I have to get a mini motorcycle or more guns," he says with a huge grin on his face.

"Girls can ride motorcycles," I tell him proudly. He dips his head to kiss me softly.

"Yeah, baby, they can and if my baby girl wants that, I will teach her," he says proudly.

"Well, why don't we get started. Vi here is a gown. Do you need any help?" Josephine asks as she hands me the gown.

"I can do it."

"Then I will give you a few moments of privacy and when you are ready, you can have Orion open the door a little and I will be right in," she explains then heads outside the room.

"She's nice," I say, then begin to undress; Orion helps me with the gown and onto the bed. "Okay, I'm ready."

"Pretty girl, I dropped a lot on you the last couple of days. You good?" Orion asks with concern.

Orion is referring to the deep conversation about his family. He was so worried about laying it all out, I could feel the anxiety and tension throughout the room even before he began. "There is nothing you can say, my grizzly, that will change how I feel about you," I tell him.

"We'll see," he says. Orion told me about his less than perfect childhood. I was shocked to know he had a brother but am excited as heck to meet him. I cried when he spoke about his mother and I could sense his pain over losing her and growing up in an emotionless house. It completed gutted me when he told me about his first wife Lisa and the loss of his child. I knew he was married before, but I had no idea that she was killed in a random shooting and I certainly didn't know that he'd lost a baby as well. He was going to have a son and that was taken from him too.

I cried endless tears at the loss and agony he went through. He lost all the warmth in his life. The nurturers were lost to him. His mom, wife and son. How much hurt can a man endure? My heart ached for him. I sat on his lap and held him close and told him how sorry I was for all that he'd endured and that I wished I had known before so I could have shouldered that burden with him.

To that, he replied, "No, baby, my life was dark before you came in and once you shone your light on me, I was terrified that I would be responsible for making that light go out too."

"Nothing that happened was your fault, honey," I told him.

"My head knows that, Vi, but I still feel it deep," he said. I could understand that.

Then to lighten the mood, I said, "Does anyone else know your name is Gavin Moore?" then it dawned on me, "Oh my God, baby Gavin is named after you?" I exclaimed in delight.

He snuck is hand up my back and into the back of my head pulling us together, so that our foreheads were touching. "Yeah baby, the brothers know my real name and yeah, baby Gavin is named after me. And absolutely a story to tell, by the way, how do you feel about the name Gabriel for a boy and Gabriella for a girl?" I threw my head back in laughter and Orion followed suit.

"I will consider it when I hear that story," I giggled.

"I gave you a lot today. Let's save that story for another day," he laughed.

"Ok, honey. Our next meeting of the minds, I need to share too," I told him. Now, laying on the table and glancing at my man, I'm anxious that what he shared might change us. "I am so glad you trust me enough to share what you have, honey. You have given me a gift and I will cherish it. I am really good, Orion," I confirm and smile.

He walks over to the door and opens it to find Josephine waiting outside. She moves to the ultrasound machine and begins to prep me with a very cool jelly on my stomach. She navigates the wand over my belly. "I spoke with the doctor and she will be in shortly. I want to reassure you that I am a nurse practitioner and have been authorized to give you the results, but the doctor will definitely be following up. If the picture is clear I can give you the sex of the baby. Are you guys ready?" she asks.

"Yeah, we both want to know," Orion says, and I nod enthusiastically.

Thump, thump, thump. "That's your baby's heartbeat." Josephine looks to us and smiles. "It's a strong heartbeat, guys. Now let's see if our peanut is going to cooperate and let us in on their secret." She continues to move the wand around. She points to the screen before us. "This is the baby's head, and here is one little hand. If you look closely you can see the other right here," she directs. "Tiny feet are right here." A pause. "Well isn't she just lovely, Mom and Dad."

"She," Orion says in a whisper.

"Yes, sir. Meet your little princess, Orion and Vi," Josephine says.

I stare at Orion as he gazes at the screen and watch as his eyes fill with silent tears. "Josephine, can you go check on the doctor?" I ask, wanting a few minutes with Orion alone.

"Of course," she says as she treks out the door.

"What are you feeling, Orion?" I ask tentatively.

"I am just thinking that I am the luckiest man on earth to have two beauties in my life," he says and bends to kiss me, slow and deep and thoroughly.

At that moment the doctor opens the door, "Am I interrupting?" Dr. Radison is smiling. "I have been told that you have been losing weight, Vi. Is that correct?"

"Yes, and I'm so tired," I tell her. Dr. Radison goes through my chart and tackles each problem one by one. Orion is asking all kinds of questions about diet and exercise. The doctor gave some pills to relieve the nausea and tackle the problem of trying to gain weight. She was very clear about keeping a stress-free environment. Dr. Radison gave a full regiment of healthy options and explained that eating smaller meals more often would be a better way to go.

By the time we were done, Orion was making a list of foods to pick up and planning walking trips for exercise.

"Is there anything else?" asks Dr. Radison.

"Sex?" I say shyly, thinking hopefully that the ban on sex can end today.

"Well, there is no reason to limit sex provided you take care. There are favorable positions for when you get bigger, Vi. I will have Josephine bring in a pamphlet on positions and what to watch for," she responds. "It's perfectly normal to find an increase in sex drive during pregnancy, Vi. Nothing to be ashamed of."

She pats my knee and heads towards the door. I look at Orion and he has a glint in his eye. "I was going to ask the same question, pretty girl. Now, I can't wait to get you home."

Risk and Demon are waiting for us outside the doctor's office. I guess they decided they didn't enjoy being ogled by a bunch of horny pregnant moment. "All good?" Risk asks.

"Yeah, bro." Orion beams with joy. "Let's get to the SUV. Then I want to get the guys on the phone." Demon is behind the wheel and Risk is dialing War's number while Orion is dialing Guard. "I assume your women are with you?" he asks

"Yea, Ava's right here with Gavin," comes from Guard.

"Right here with Maddie," pipes in War.

"Go ahead, babe, tell our family," Orion says. He wants me to share our news.

"Well, Orion and I would like you all to be available on or around December 1st to meet our baby girl, Gabriella Moore," I say loudly. The car is filled with hooting and hollering, showcasing the excitement for our baby girl's arrival.

Then I hear Guard, "Vi, you don't have to—"

I cut him off quickly.

"I don't know it all yet, Guard, but I trust that this is right. Thank you for bringing him to me," I tell him.

"Okay, I want to get Vi home to rest. We will talk with you all later," Orion says.

Risk and Demon follow us through the front door. We picked up take out on our way back. I manage to keep down half a turkey sandwich and a few chips. Orion makes sure I am comfortable on the couch with water, my phone, converter and snacks close at hand before he tells me he needs to head out for a bit.

"Everything okay, honey?" I ask

"Perfect. Risk is staying with you. I will be back soon," he says and kisses me sweetly. "Rest up, pretty girl. I am going to explore every part of your luscious body later tonight," he whispers in my ear.

I watch my man saunter out the door. He looks amazing with his broad shoulders and amazing ass. I know that Orion works out to stay fit. We have worked out together in the past. I loved it. He always pushed me to work a little harder and taught me the right way to lift weights and made sure to spot me so I wouldn't hurt myself.

The morning activities wore me out. I'm exhausted. I decide to lay my head down just for a minute. I'm drifting off when I hear Risk utter, "Sleep little momma. I am here and you are safe." Then I feel my wrap slide over and envelop me.

I wake to the rustling of paper and bags, bringing me out of my sleep. I blink a few times, allowing my eyes to adjust to the light in the room. I sit up and rub my eyes. The room is full, with bags and packages lining the counter and table.

I look around and see that Orion is closing the front door and securing the latch as Risk leaves.

I stand and walk over to the bags. "What's all of

this?" I can't believe that Orion went out all by himself to let me know his excitement about having a baby girl. I love his excitement.

Orion approaches and begins to pull out pink baby clothes. There are pink and lace booties, pink onesies, pink dresses and shoes. Baby rattles, bibs, stuffies, a teddy bear, and yes, it's all pink. Then he reaches for a box with an elegant designer logo. "Open it," he says smoothly.

I slowly lift the lid and pull back the pink and silver tissue paper. I lift a black leather jacket with sequin pink and silver writing on the back. *Baby Pride* it reads. I throw my head back in laughter and hug Orion close. I look around the room and view a sea of pink and glitter.

"This is perfect, honey," I tell him as I lift the jacket to my chest and hold it close.

"I want you to have it all, Vi. You and Gabriella will never have to worry."

"All we need is you, Orion."

He touches my cheek and his hand glides down, over my back and cups my ass. "The ban has been lifted, pretty girl. You can show me how much you want me by stripping down and letting me love you."

I set the jacket down at walk towards the doorway to the bedroom, look over my shoulder and smile suggestively. "Are you coming?" I say.

I hear the thunder of his feet running towards me, and screech in surprise. Orion lifts me in a romantic bridal hold as he walks us through the threshold and struts to the bed.

CHAPTER 14

We'll make it perfect!

Orion

Baby, we've been to a handful of decent places and you want to make this place our home?" I ask is disbelief, thinking that Vi has lost her mind. As she walks around the room with the floorboards creaking, I am tempted to pull her out of here, terrified of her moving about the room and having the ground caving in. The walls need new drywall, the kitchen and bathrooms need to be gutted and God only knows what condition the roof is in. Yet, here she stands, looking out the window to the backyard. It is vast and impressive; however, it is the only thing about this house that is worth looking at. It backs onto trees and I know that Vi loves that.

Her expression of tranquility rivals that of her

intense pleasure from our previous evening. Last night I took my time revving up my girl until she begged me to come inside her. With supreme human control, I paid homage to her body. From the moment I lay her down on the bed, I began to strip her slowly, as if I was unwrapping the most perfect gift and wanted to revel in the excitement as I removed each layer.

I made her watch me love her. Her eyes never left me. Vi reached for my cock and I stopped her immediately. No way I had that kind of resolve and I wanted this to go slow. We have time after the baby arrives to fuck hard and long. Last night I wanted to give us both what we needed and take care of my woman as she deserved. I tortured her with my mouth, my tongue lavishing her breasts until she begged me to stop. Of course, I obeyed and continued my decent to her navel and circled it over and over before making my way over to her hip bone where she squirmed beneath me as I hit a sensitive spot. I love that low mewl that erupts from her lips whenever I hit that spot. I held her still as she watched me move lower. Her hands grabbed my hair and I lifted my gaze to meet hers as I licked her clit over and over, circling it, flicking and nipping until she was desperate.

"Please, grizzly, I need you," she begged. "I need you inside me." I spread her wider, kissing the inside of her thighs, one then the other, and finally one long last lick along her pussy as she lifted her hips and moaned sweetly. I lifted my body over hers, took her hands and entwined them in mine, placing them on either side of her head as I entered her. Inch by inch. Listening to every moan, pant and mewl that emitted from my Vi. I was fully inside her, my eyes never

WE'LL MAKE IT PERFECT!

leaving hers. "I love you, Vi," I said. With every stroke, a new mewl erupted.

"Love you, too, baby. Everything that you are," she said panting. Her cunt gripped me, letting me know that she was close. I went faster and harder, still looking to be gentle but firm.

"Every. Thing. That. You. Are," I told her with every stroke. I heard her orgasm rip through her, and I followed suit. She lay exhausted in my arms with that smile on her face. Much like the one she holds now, no less beautiful as she peers out the window looking at our potential new yard.

"I had this once," she says as she tuns to me.

"What?" I asked, confused.

"My father took off the day my mother told him she was pregnant. I have never met him and have no desire to do so. My mom tried to be a mom. She made sure I was clean, had food, and a toy or two. It's all she could afford. I was good with that," she explains. A heavy sigh escapes her lips, "Then she met Aaron. At first, he was good with me but eventually he didn't like sharing my mother's attention. I don't blame her for choosing Aaron; she suffered with ratty jobs and making do, and Aaron could give her anything she wanted. Mom took me to my grandparents. Nana and Popi were wonderful to me and gave me all that I might need. I had the most wonderful yard and Popi put up a tire swing where I would sit and swing and he would sit and tell me stories. Nana made me pretty dresses and showed me how to sew. I laughed a lot. I mean I missed my mom, but I decided that she deserved to be happy too, so I let her go."

She approaches me cautiously, seeing that my

face is fuming mad. What woman chooses a man over her own daughter? And what kind of asshole would force a woman to make that choice?

"I had a good life, Orion. The only time I hurt was when they passed. Popi died from heart failure when I was sixteen. That's when I decided I needed to work to help Nana. She was devasted by his death and Popi did most of the banking, paying bills and such. I got a job at the local diner and loved it. I got to meet new people every day. I was good at it and got killer tips," she smirks and places her arms around my waist. "I left that town when Nana passed. I was eighteen. I truly think she died of a broken heart because she missed Popi so much. She always said that there was a whole world I needed to see, and I wanted to see it. I had nothing to tie me to that town. No real friends, no family, so why not, I thought. I have been to a few places and I liked them all. When I reached our town, I knew I'd found home. Molly was amazing to take me in, the girls actually invite me out with them. I found happy here. Then you came and I thought there was nothing more perfect than what I was living," she finishes.

I was still upset to know what she went through. She was taking care of her grandma at sixteen. Waiting tables and roaming towns to find a place that felt like home.

"I am glad you have good memories, babe, but I am not happy that a woman left her kid for a man. I am even more pissed that you've been moving around looking for happy. And now that I have my head on straight, I am going to make sure that happy is here to stay." I kiss her nose and her face softens.

WE'LL MAKE IT PERFECT!

"This house may not be perfect, but Maddie and War are across the way, Ava and Guard are less than ten minutes up the road and the compound is less than twenty minutes from here. Our family is here, our baby girl will have people around to love and care for her. And we will too," she says joyfully. "I know it's a lot of work, but I am handy and can help." Then she pulls out of my arms and grabs my hand, tugging me through the house.

She pulls me down the hall to the master suite. "We can decorate in a soft grey and deep blue. The big windows bring in tons of light and we can put a big armchair right here," she points near the window, "and a king size bed, here," she continues. Then she takes me into the room next to it. "Gabriella's room is big enough to fit all the toys and crib, although with all the clothes you bought her, we are going to have to add another closet," she teases. She starts to pull me into yet another room and I pull her back.

"Pretty girl, if this is the house you want, then this is the house you get. I know you are thinking of me being close to my brothers. I am positive that Ava and Maddie will be over all the time to help out," I tell her and hold her in my arms. "Hear me, baby. No more working at Molly's. You work on your jewelry and make yourself happy. You take care of our baby and I will take care of both of you."

She leaps into my arms forcing me to lift her as she wraps her legs around my waist, wrapping her arms around my neck, her nose touching mine. "We'll make this place perfect. You and me, Orion."

With that, I take her mouth in a deep kiss, then let her down to find the real estate agent outside to seal the deal. Then I need to get Risk on the phone to develop plans to get this place livable. I want it done fast. The drive to and from Hanna's is too long from the crew and I have an uneasy feeling that something is not right around that neighbourhood. I don't like leaving Vi there on her own.

CHAPTER 15

Revolving Door

Vi

Three months later

"Ava, can you put the blue colour swatch next to the dove grey tile?" I ask. We are in the final stages of renovating the house. Risk has done a marvelous job of creating a design that maximized the space in the house. He somehow managed to add extra storage in places I never would have thought of. He is so talented. I have seen the work he created in Maddie's studio and had no doubts about him taking over the construction at our place. All that needs to be done is the final touches in the kitchen and adding the appliances. The big decision I have been negotiated internally has been the master bathroom. Each time I ask Orion, I get the same response, "Don't give a fuck, baby, as long as you and Gabriella are there when I walk in."

Maddie and Ava are great sounding boards. They have helped me in choosing the baby's room colours and furniture. We went with soft peach and cream tones. One wall has a mural of baby zoo animals in carton figures, all giggling and happy, tousling around in the grass.

I keep going back and forth on the tile, my final decision, and if I can finally make up my mind our home can be complete in less than two weeks. I am getting bigger and gaining weight. My last couple of appointments with the doctor went really well; she was pleased with my progress. Not to mention that Orion has been over the moon that I'm keeping down my meals and making some craving requests. Two in the morning sundaes have become a thing for me. Orion's reaction is simply, "Babe," then a sigh. He called one of the recruits and within a half hour, a sundae shows up at the door.

"Vi, I think you want to go with the lighter grey," Maddie says. "It will still have the grey to tie in the bedroom and you will be able to make the room look brighter. The darker grey will make it gloomier and more serious."

"I guess," I say uncertainly.

"Doll, this is the last thing you need to decide on for a while and then we can plan your baby shower," Ava says.

I bite my lower lip, unwilling to make the choice.

"What has you looking like that?" I hear Orion

ask. He must have come in the screen door. For a big man, he can be very quiet.

"Tiles," I say. He knows what I mean. I have been going back and forth for two days.

"This one," he points to the one Maddie had picked with the light grey and hues of cream white.

"Are you sure?" I ask. "Are you just saying that one," I point, "so I don't hold up construction?" I narrow my eyes.

He throws back his head and laughs. "Yes. I also think that it will look really good when we are done," he responds honestly.

"Ugh! Okay that one and get all these samples away from me before I start changing my mind," I say, tossing my hands in the air. I am glad he made that decision. It was all becoming too much. I am feeling heavy and swollen. I haven't been spending the time I want on my business and I was getting cranky.

I push myself off the edge of the sofa and begin to wander over to my worktable. I see the orders from the specialty shops and my anxiety start to climb again. I pick up the email with the details, furrowing my brows with concern.

"I don't know if I can get this all done," I cry, silent tears beginning to fall down my face. "I have worked so hard to get more orders and I can't get them done. Between the house, feeling sick and being exhausted, I am letting down the stores that have supported me." A flood of emotion moves through me and I can't seem to contain my tears.

Ava and Maddie are quick to their feet, but Orion already has his arms around me. "Shhh, Vi. We can get you some extra help."

"I can't have you guys fixing everything," I continue to cry.

"Why not, honey?" asks Ava.

"Because one day I will use up all your love for me and you won't want me here anymore," I say in a full on sob.

Maddie approaches and pulls me out of Orion's embrace. She leads me to the kitchen and sits me down before sitting opposite me. In her sweet, calm voice, she proceeds to read me the riot act. "Now listen here, Vi, I love you like a sister. Ava loves you like a sister. We are here because we want to be part of your life. You have given to each and every person you have met. Whether it was for a moment by serving a coffee or for years by supporting, and guiding others. Do not think that Ava has forgotten how lonely she was when she first got here. How you took her by the hand and taught her the ins and outs of being part of the Lady Pride. She adores you. Gavin thinks you're the bomb. He reaches for you the minute you walk into the room because he knows goodness when he feels it. Nothing more pure than a child's love, Vi. The brotherhood searched endlessly and without complaint. They missed you. YOU, Vi! Simply because you are who you are." Her voice cracks. "I cannot even begin to tell you how much you mean to me. You saved my life. You kept my secrets and allowed me to grow into the me I am because you taught me to be free." Maddie takes a deep breath before continuing. "Allow us to give a little back. You aren't in this alone. Ava let you guide her. I let you free me. Let us all be part of the world you deserve."

She squeezes my hands and we are both sobbing quietly. Ava approaches us, sobbing as well, pulling another chair close and grabbing a hand from the both of us.

We all hear Orion at the doorway. "Apparently the women have had a meeting and we are going to need some help to get Vi's orders out." There's a pause before he continues. "I have three blubbering females here and a problem to solve. I don't think we are going to be much use at making the shit they are putting together but we can pack it and get it mailed out."

A few minutes go by and Orion is pacing the room, making plans with someone I assume is Guard. He finally snaps his phone away and turns back to us.

"Vi, give the ladies instructions on what they can do to get things moving. We have reinforcements coming. The guys will pack what you have ready and get it out today. What timeframe do you think we need to get the order out and get you caught up?" he asks, exhibiting an extremely attractive take charge attitude. I guess bossy is the new sexy when you see Orion do it!

"I think we can get the bracelets done today and half of the necklaces. Tomorrow we can tackle the rest of the necklaces. But I would need at least one more day to get the shoe buckles and belts done. That would be working a full day like from eight in the morning to into the late evening," I say blinking away my tears.

"I'm in," pipes in Ava. "Ditto," says Maddie. They are both racing over to the table.

"Let's go, girl, we have a business to run," Ava commands.

"I am going out to get some packing boxes and whatever other supplies we need. Write that shit out. Risk is staying at the house to finish with the workmen. Guard has a meeting with other crews and is taking War with him. That means that Gavin, Ava, and Maddie stay here for the next few days. Whoever else is available will be coming in shifts to help. The prospects will be supplying meals. Let Cris know what you want," Orion lays out.

A plan has been formed. Ava and Maddie are pulling up chairs at the worktable. I gather my thoughts. We can do this. If I can get these orders out, then I can spend the rest of my time getting ahead of the game so I can spend more time recovering after the baby arrives. I pull out the beads and place them in pertinent piles based on product. I give the girls direction and will place my final spin on the designs after the basics have been dealt with.

Three Days Later

True to their word, the gang has done all they can to get me through. Not one complaint. The guys packed and hauled according to the packing slips I printed. Ava and Maddie assisted with the basic placing of gems on the appropriate pieces. I then took time with each piece to create the look and feel that guided me. *Vi-Vacious Designs* is meant to be one-of-a-kind artistic pieces with elegance.

Guard and War picked up their women and baby Gavin an hour ago. I am finishing my last piece and Orion is in the kitchen making dinner. That's right—making dinner. He has never cooked for me before. Spaghetti and meatballs. He is making the sauce from scratch. The meatballs too. I didn't know he could cook. Most of the time we've been together, we would eat out or do takeout.

REVOLVING DOOR

In the last three months, he has been more open to talking about anything and everything, except club business, which I know is never leaving the club. I can live with that. I trust that if something was going to affect me or the baby, Orion would protect us.

After my outburst about using up their love, Orion decided that I must still had shit from my past to get out. He let me have my space. I knew he was worried because he has been keeping a closer eye and has been very watchful. I catch him looking at me, searching my face. I'm not sure where that came from. Orion says that although I had my grandparents, I could still be harboring feeling of abandonment. I think it's plain and simple. I have never mattered to anyone else; I only had myself to rely on. I didn't think anyone else would want to be part of my problems. I was clearly wrong.

The doorbell rings as I am putting away the last of the tools. "I'll get it," I say.

"Kay," I hear from the kitchen. "Look through the window to see who it is first."

Did I mention Orion is bossy!?

Hanna is standing at the front door, holding a box of what I can only imagine are lemon squares. I swing the door open to let her in. I haven't seen her for over a week.

"Hi Hanna! I've missed you," I tell her, and haul her in for a hug.

Hanna gives me a shy smile. "Me or my lemon squares?" she asks cheekily.

"Can I say both, so I don't get in trouble?" I laugh. "Come on in. After all, this is your house," I remind her.

"Oh, Vi, it's yours until you are ready to leave," Hanna replies as she steps through. I lead her into the kitchen. "Orion is cooking," I tell her.

"I can see that." She turns to him. "Hi Orion."

"Good to see you, Hanna," Orion replies.

"I brought you both your favorites. I know you have been busy with the house and haven't had a chance to come into the bakery. I brought lemon squares for Vi, and for you, Orion, chocolate éclair bites," Hanna lifts the lid and my mouth begins to water. "And in this box is a variety for you to take to the guys working on your home—for added incentive."

"They look amazing, Hanna. And I'm sure that they taste even better," I tell her.

"Dinner is ready, Vi. Set another place for Hanna and I'll dish it out," Orion growls. He must be hungry.

"I don't want to interrupt. I just wanted to drop these off," Hanna says.

"You're here and we're eating," Orion barks. "That's your seat." Hanna is so surprised at his insistence that she takes the seat indicated.

Dinner is light and fun. Orion gets Hanna talking about the bakery and how she came up with her special recipes. The conversation is light and easy. Hanna giggles at the mock bickering between Orion and me. I tell her about how everyone helped with the last order and how excited I am to be caught up.

"I would have helped too," she offers.

"Thank you, Hanna. You have already given me a home, and an endless supply of lemon treats," I remind her. "But I will keep you in mind for next time. And that's a promise."

A crash outside throws Orion out of his seat and

his chair clattering to the floor as he runs to the front window. Hanna and I follow quickly on his heels. We see a car pulling away from Hanna's car. The driver had hit her vehicle and was now tearing away from the scene. The look of horror on Hanna's face is apparent.

Orion runs after the car, probably to see if he can get a glimpse of the driver or the license plate. He runs back to us and approaches Hanna, asking, "Who was that Hanna?" His voice is gruff. To say he's pissed would be putting it mildly.

She shakes her head, not saying a word. Her hands are shaking, and her eyes are wide. She's scared. I know scared. Mostly because I have felt that emotion a ton in my life; I recognize the fear.

Orion takes her by the shoulders and holds her steady. "Hanna. Focus," he commands.

She looks up at him.

"Hanna, who was that?" he asks more quietly. He is gentling his tone to soothe her.

"I'm not sure," she whispers.

"Not sure?" Orion repeats.

"I, um… it, um, it might be my ex," she whispers. "I don't know why he would come here though. He knows I don't live here."

"What's going on?" I ask her quietly. She turns away from Orion to face me. Her face is red, and I can see her embarrassment.

"I should go," she says.

"You can't drive that, Hanna. Go have a seat and keep Vi company. I am going to get someone to come get your car and drive you home," Orion states.

I guide Hanna to the couch then move to the

kitchen to grab her a cup of coffee. I hear Orion on the phone.

"The shithead plowed right into her car, with definite purpose. He came here for that. Don't know what the fuck is going on, but she is freaked," Orion says. "Yeah, she needs to be driven home. I am not leaving Vi here alone." Then, "Okay send the tow and get her a ride. She needs an eye. Get someone to keep watch on her. I don't trust that this is over." He pauses while whoever is on the other end talks. "Risk, we need the house finished fast. I need to get Vi out of here."

I walk back to Hanna.

"I'm so sorry, Vi. I didn't mean to ruin your night." She is having a hard time meeting my eyes. There is so much more to this story; I can feel it.

I am about to reassure her when the doorbell rings again. It can't possibly be Risk yet.

"Stay put," I hear Orion's growl as he strolls to the door. He pulls the door open and although he is blocking my view, I hear a familiar voice.

"I am looking for Vivianna Roslan. I was told I could find her here." It's a male voice. I know I've heard it before but can't place it. It's a low voice and he articulates his words very clearly. Definitely sounds refined.

"Who are you?" Orion's patience is wearing thin. He is being terse and curt.

"I'm not sure that is any business of yours. I am looking for a moment of Vivianna's time," the voice bites back.

"Listen, man, no clue who you are, and I don't give a fuck, but no one, and I mean no one gets to Vi without getting through me first. So, I suggest you tell me who you are, and I can see if you are welcome here," Orion says, reaffirming his stance. I try to look around him, but Orion's huge frame blocks everything but the stranger's shoes. They are black, shiny, and high-end tailored shoes.

"Alright then, could you please let Vivianna know that Aaron Morgan requests a moment of her time," he says. With that I jump, well try to jump; my bulging belly is making it harder and harder to get in and out of the soft plush seat. Automatically, Hanna rises to help me out of my chair.

"Oh, hell no!" I hear Orion roar.

I race to the door. Aaron comes into view as he hears me moving towards them. "Vi, slow down, and come here to me," Orion commands.

I slow my steps and come to stand next to him. He quickly places his arm protectively around my waist and arranges my body next his so that we are touching. I gaze up at Orion and can see that he is not pleased by the presence of my stepfather on our doorstep. I place my hand on his chest to reassure him. He looks down at me with a grim expression.

"Vivianna?" Aaronn asks as his eyes move from my face to my baby belly and then back up again.

"Hello Aaron," I greet him smoothly. "This is an unexpected surprise. How did you know where to find me? Is Mom alright?" Aaron and my mom disappeared from my life when I was five-years-old. They dropped me off at my grandparents where Mom explained that they were better equipped to look after me and that she needed to look after Aaron. They didn't return for Christmases, birthdays, my high school graduation; they didn't return for either of my grandparents' funerals and when it was time to sell their home, they sent a proxy with authority to sign over the proceeds to me. That was the only kindness they had shown me. Essentially, I have not seen either of them since they left over twenty-five years ago and now that Aaron is standing before me, I am wondering where my mother is.

"I would prefer to speak with you inside, Vivianna, and not on a stoop where all the neighbours can hear our business." Well it's obvious that his pompous attitude hasn't changed in the slightest.

"Drop the attitude, asshole," Orion says. "You came to us."

Aaron releases a heavy sigh. "Vivianna, your mother needs your assistance and I have come to take you to her so that we can discuss this fully. Although, I was unaware that you are with child. I am not sure how this will affect the outcome," Aaron states. He thinks it is a forgone conclusion that I'll put on my shoes and coat and prance out the door to his car for a family drive to reconnect with my mother.

"Not happening," Orion growls. "Vi goes nowhere without me. As you can see Vi is pregnant with our daughter and has enough to deal with. Her mother wants to see her, she can come to her."

"That's not possible," Aaron says through clenched teeth.

"Just a minute Aaron," I tell him and pull Orion further into the hallway.

"I need to know what's going on," tell Orion. I look at him and he sees I am anxious and need to know what's happening with my mom.

"He comes in, he sits, he talks. We listen. You do

not leave here with him and after he speaks his piece, we sit down and discuss it." I can sense all Orion wants to do is slam the door in his face and this is his way of compromising.

"Absolutely," I reassure him.

He walks back to the front. "Come in and have a seat on the couch," he says to Aaron.

Hanna is standing as we make our way into the room.

"I can wait outside," she says. Hanna is very perceptive and sees the uneasiness in Aaron's demeanor.

"No, Hanna. But why don't you go make us a fresh pot of coffee," Orion asks quietly.

"Okay," she replies and slides out of the room to enter the kitchen.

I am careful as I sit in the chair across from Aaron. "Now, what can I do for you Aaron?" I feel Orion's presence behind me and feel his hand at the nape of my neck, letting me know that I am not alone.

Aaron runs his hands over his face and explodes. "Marie is ill. She has been ill for quite a while, but it wasn't until six months ago that she was diagnosed. The cancer surgery and treatment have taken a toll on her. The doctors have her stable for the time being and she is in remission at least for now. Her mind though, isn't healing."

I feel my stomach drop and a whoosh of air leaves my lungs. I gasp for air and cover my mouth.

"Babe," Orion's gentle tone has me turn. He is kneeling on one knee and is taking my hands in his. "Breathe, pretty girl. Look at me. That's right, just breathe with me," he guides me through the shock.

Once I gather some semblance of control, my

eyes revert back to Aaron. "What do you mean, her mind isn't healing?" I ask. Mom had cancer and I never knew. No one bothered to come get me to let me know. I'm letting all this information sink in. Now I am getting irritated.

"Marie had breast cancer. She has undergone treatment. She has had her breast removed and has gone through chemotherapy and radiation. She is physically on the mend, but I can't get her to come back to how we were," he confides. "She is saying that she deserves to be sick. She has earned the loss of her breast. This is penance for how she treated you. Because she chose me over you," he croaks.

I blink at his words.

"You and Marie royally fucked up," I hear Orion state plainly.

I glance at him, my expression stern. "Orion," I whisper and shake my head, letting him know this is not the way I want to handle this.

"Look, I know that I was an asshole for making her choose me over her daughter. I couldn't handle a kid. I tried; I don't know if you can remember but I really tried at the beginning," he pleads, and I nod in agreement. "It was never about you, Vivianna. I would come over and Marie was tired from working and making your dinner and playing with you, giving you a bath and repeat. Every day was the same. At first, we were going to take a couple of months to just be together and then come and get you and we could be a family. Then the days passed, and we were happy to have that time. One day passed, then another, and another, until finally, we looked back and convinced ourselves that you were settled with your grandparents. "

"That's bullshit, and you know it!" roared Orion. "That fucking excuse is pathetic."

"Easy, grizzly," I say quietly and pat his hand, resting on my knee.

"Aaron, why is it that you're here?" I ask. "It can't be to reminisce about the good old days because you didn't allow me to be part of those days with Mom. Is it guilt?" I quirk my head to the side. "Did she send you?"

"Marie has no idea that I'm here. I'm to blame for the past. I was selfish and love her so much that I wanted her all to myself. I see that I have caused her so much pain and I never wanted that for her. I didn't know how much I hurt her until this happened and she is killing herself slowly with the guilt of having left you" Now he is sobbing. "I love her. I can't watch her do this to herself. I know I have no right to ask but I am asking for Marie and not me. Please come and talk to her. If you forgive her, maybe she can forgive herself."

"Oh, hell no!" Orion roars again. The yelling brings Hanna back into the room. At the same time the doorbell rings again. "For fuck's sake!" Orion bellows.

"I can get it," says Hanna.

"Hanna, come here and stay next to Vi." Orion turns to Aaron as he rises from his haunches, "Not another word until I get back." He strides to the door to find Risk and Cris standing on the other side.

"Hey—"Risk begins but is interrupted by Orion.

"Get in here and lock the door," he cuts them off and returns to my side.

"Pretty girl, I need a few words with my brothers. Be back in two minutes," he says as he places a kiss on my forehead and directs Risk and Cris into the kitchen.

"Will you come?" Aaron asks quietly as soon as Orion is out of sight.

I am utterly confused as to what to feel. I am sad that no one thought to contact me when my mom was first going through all of this, angry that they left me, truly pissed off that Aaron deigns to make the effort to appease his guilt through getting me to do as he wants and more upset at myself for wanting to see my mom even if it is for her benefit. I never expected to be contacted by either of them ever again. As far as I was concerned, I have been an orphan since Nanna and Popi's deaths. I accepted that and moved on to find my new brand of happiness here with Orion.

A short time later, Risk and Orion return. Cris takes a step back to stand next to them.

"Come on, Hanna, you're with me," Risk says as he reenters the room. "Give your keys to Cris. He is going to get your car into the shop and get it looked after." Risk holds out a hand for her to take. Hanna tentatively places her hand in his and walks towards the front door.

"I'll call you Vi. If you need anything, please call me, anytime," Hanna says sweetly.

"Calling Guard as soon as I leave here to fill him in. Expect a call," Risk says. Cris stays quiet but is giving Aaron a guarded once over. I know Cris well and that look would intimidate me.

It's now back to the three of us. "Here's how this is going to go Aaron; you are going to leave. Vi and I are going to sit down and sift through this information. Leave us your number and we will get back to you in the morning," Orion explains.

"Will you call?" he asks, not convinced that he will hear from either of us again.

"Orion is a man of his word. And I have always kept my promises," I retaliate. "I did not leave my child to be raised by someone else." I am getting a headache. Orion is so perceptive he appears to sense it.

"We're done for now. Write your number on the pad in front of you. Vi has had a long day and she needs her rest." He points to the pad on the coffee table.

Understanding that this conversation is at an impasse, Aaron jots down his number and rises to leave. With a final, "Please," he closes the door behind him.

"Baby, I am going to lock down the house. Get ready for bed and we will talk it out," Orion whispers in my ear. I nod and with his help, make my way to bed.

My head is still reeling from working all hours to get my orders out the door, Hanna's crash and crazy ex, and seeing Aaron after all these years with crappy news about my mom. I wash my face, going through my routine all the while wondering what I would say to my mother.

Orion finds me in the bathroom, staring at my reflection in the mirror. Silently he leads me to bed and tucks me in, climbing in behind me. He has me cradled on my side, spooning me.

"Pretty girl, it's been a heavy day and an even heavier night. How are you doing?" he says as he caresses my hair and pulls it back from my eyes as he nuzzles closer.

"I don't know how I feel. I mean, I feel everything. I'm mad, sad, pissed, confused," I whisper back.

"No decisions tonight, baby," he kisses my cheek. "Sleep. I am here and together we will figure this out."

"Just a thought, honey, but I think we should install a revolving door," I joke. I can feel Orion's body shake with laughter behind me.

"We're moving, babe, not spending that money," he said. I lay awake feeling his warmth until I eventually feel my mind and body relax into a much-required slumber.

CHAPTER 16

Moving on

Orion

The road is lined with tall maple trees. The colour of the leaves has started to turn as we are heading into autumn. It's Vi's favorite time of year. Since I've known her, she has planted herself in the park to watch the leaves. She says that it's calming. A process, she says. The cycle of seasons and each season brings its own special beauty. I didn't get it then.

I glance over to see her biting her lower lip. She's worried about seeing her mother again. I am still unsure about this family reunion. I don't think Vi owes these people a damn thing. I can't get over the fact that they dumped her on her grandparents and tore off into the sunset to be happy. I know Aaron had money. I checked out his background the next day. He owns a distribution warehouse and has done well for himself. They never sent a dime to her grandmother after her husband died and Vi ended up having to leave school and pay bills. Marie never worked after meeting Aaron and has spent her time volunteering. Volunteering! Probably to appease her guilty conscious.

Vi is a bundle of nerves. We went back and forth on the decision and ultimately decided that she needed to see this through. She has valid reasoning. She has questions she wants answers to. The killer was that she didn't want to have any regrets. I have lived a life of regrets and never want Vi to feel what I've felt.

Ava called this morning to ask if she needed moral support, followed by Maddie, then Hanna. Vi politely refused but told them to be on standby for when she came home because she had no idea how this was going to go.

We've reached the end of the drive. I notice her hand shaking. I take it in mine, "We don't have to go in," I tell her. At that moment, Aaron comes to the front door. She raises her head to the door as she hears the creaking of the hinge.

"Yes, I do. I need to see this through." She raises her eyes to mine. "Thank you for being with me."

"Nowhere else I would rather be, pretty girl." I smile at her. "Where my girls go, I go." I touch her cheek and am rewarded with her brilliant smile. "You ready or you want me to drive around the block a few times?" I ask teasingly.

"Ready." I get out and stalk to Vi's door, helping her out of the car. I see that Aaron is agitated. He hasn't told his wife of this visit and is taking a chance that this will bring Marie back from the edge. When I called him the other day to inform him that we would make the trip, he informed me that he didn't want to tell Marie in case Vi changes her mind and didn't want Marie agonizing over the meeting. Despite him being a complete dick with Vi, it seems like he truly loves his wife.

Vi is now beginning to walk more slowly and waddles ever so slightly. She has become clumsier lately so she is always holding on to me when she is up and about. Her health has greatly improved and is on track for weight.

"Thank you for coming," Aaron says genuinely. He opens the door wider to allow us entry. The house is neat, pristine actually. The furniture is solid and of excellent quality. The place is filled with antiques. They have definitely lived well.

He guides us down the corridor to a sitting room. I am stunned to see a more mature version of Vi. Marie is petite with the same red tones in her hair. She wears her hair in a bun but definitely the same colour. They have the same cheekbones and lips. Marie's eyes are blue and under her eyes are dark circles. Either from the illness or guilt or maybe both.

When she sees Vi, her mouth drops open, and tears well up in her eyes. I can see she wants to reach out to her but is afraid of rejection. I look at Vi and see the same reaction.

"Baby, she's waiting for you," I say, stepping further into the room, leading her towards Marie. Marie tries to stand but must still be pretty weak as she stumbles. I release Vi and reach out to steady her.

"Thank you, young man," she says quietly. I see it. Regret. Pain.

"Are you okay?" Vi asks.

"I'm afraid to touch you. I might wake up and you'll be gone," Marie says.

Aaron brings an armchair closer to Vi. "Please sit, Vi." He then turns to Marie. "Honey, please sit back down. Doctor said you need to rest." He guides Marie back into her chair as I help Vi get comfortable.

"I'll get us some coffee," Aaron says and removes himself from the room.

No way I'm leaving Vi yet.

"I hear you've been sick, Mom. You need to rest and get better," Vi says quietly, reaching out a hand, placing it over top of her mother's, which is resting on the arm of the chair. Her mother looks down at her daughter's hand and bursts into tears.

"I'm so sorry, Vi. I don't deserve you," she cries. "I deserve to be sick. I was so selfish. I left you. I loved you and I still left you. I'm a horrible person. A horrible mother." Marie is sobbing uncontrollably. Vi is now weeping silent tears as well.

I hand Marie some tissues. "Marie, you can sit here and cry or you can speak with your daughter and make peace so that you can both move forward." I lay it out as I see it. I personally think they don't deserve a second chance but Vi needs to see this through and I will do anything for her.

"Mom, Orion's right. I just want to know why. Why did you walk away?" Vi asks.

Marie's breathing settles. "Vivianna, I wanted to give you everything. I worked and then worked some more, and I could barely feed us. Then Aaron came along and helped out. I'm not sure if you remember but he used to buy you toys and teach you the alphabet. You liked him and he loved me. I thought we had found our happily ever after. Our lives were about taking care of you. We were adjusting to try and be a family and Aaron lived alone all his life and was having trouble adjusting. He suggested that we leave you with mom and dad for just a couple of months during the summer so we could spend quality time together and then pick you up and start fresh. I thought it was a great idea. It gave me time with Aaron alone and then we would come back. The intention was to always come back," she says adamantly.

"But you didn't, Mom," Vi prods.

With a heavy sigh, Marie replies, "You're right. We didn't. We got married, then went on a honeymoon. We decided to buy the right house for the family, then Aaron wanted to make sure that his business was doing well to be able to take care of us. We always had an excuse. The truth is, I was afraid to take you back."

"I was five. How can you be afraid of a five-year-old girl who thought her mom gave up on her because she was worthless?" Vi spews.

"My baby girl, you were so perfect, and I was not. When I am with Aaron, he thinks I am everything. When I was with you, I felt like I could do nothing right. I'm not saying it's your fault. I know it was mine. I was a coward and I missed out on a life that included you," she sobs.

Aaron is leaning against the wall, watching this all unfold. His face is pale and anguished.

"Where do we go from here?" I pipe up and look around at the three family members. "And let me begin by saying both you and Aaron have to earn our trust. I have watched Vi tear herself up wondering who else she was going to lose because you walked out on her when she was a kid. She is having my daughter and no one and nothing is more important to me than Vi and my baby girl."

"I can see you found yourself a very protective man," Marie said.

"He is the most amazing man, Mom. He's everything I have ever wanted," Vi replies.

I bend down to Vi's ear and whisper, "You keep talking like that and I am going to kiss you senseless."

"Right," she whispers back.

I stand and look at Aaron. "Let's leave them alone for a bit. Why don't you show me around the place?" My thought is to get Aaron alone to see what his play is here. Vi is not moving closer or looking after her mother. She has enough on her plate. Aaron came to find us in desperation and desperate men do not always have the best intentions.

"Yeah, sure," he replies. "Vi, please see that she stays sitting. She hasn't been following doctor's orders and she needs to rest."

Once I get Aaron outside, I waste no time in setting things straight. "Ok, Aaron, you appear out of nowhere and drop a bomb on Vi, then you sit at the back of the room and watch the two of them without saying a word. What the fuck do you want?"

"I want Marie to be happy. She has suffered for so long. I love her more than anything and I couldn't do anything to help her. So, I did the only thing I could, which was to find Vi and pray like hell that she would have enough love left for her mother to come and see her," Aaron says calmly. "I fucked up. I wish I could go back and do it over, but I can't. Marie is everything to me." His voice cracks.

"Vi is everything to me. Know this now: Marie and you will be welcome if and when Vi and I allow it. We lead our lives and maybe with time, if you get the invite, don't be stupid, take the invite. My woman and *my child,*" I stress, "come first."

"I understand." He nods. "Marie will want to see her grandchild and I will too."

"We'll cross that bridge. Right now, we are day by day. I warn you, Aaron, you mess with Vi, my kid, or me and I will make sure you pay dearly. I will not hold back, and I will make you suffer. You interfered once with their lives; you will not do it again," I force through my teeth.

"Understood, but just so you know, I only want what's best for my wife," Aaron says quietly.

We make our way back to the ladies, where they are sipping coffee. "Vi, one coffee a day, the doctor said."

She giggles. "Relax, honey, it's decaf."

She seems good. Marie looks better. I am not convinced, but then again, I am a harder nut to crack. I don't forgive easy, especially where Vi is involved. We are moving forward. Making a home, growing our family. I will ride it out to see if Marie and Aaron have a place in it. For now, I will revel in watching Vi giggle.

CHAPTER 17

Let me love you

Vi

I am so nervous. I think I am more nervous today than I was when I saw Mom and Aaron after years and years of no contact. I want Nate to like me.

Last night, Orion told me it doesn't matter if he does or doesn't because he has never followed family rules and although he loves his brother, he loves me more. I reflect on the previous night. It was magical.

After those words, I went to great lengths to show him how much I adored him. Even with my massive baby bump, I was able to find a satin baby doll teddy with an empire waist, in emerald green with black lace trim.

Orion always goes through the same motions, night after night, locking down the house. I would say he's paranoid but after all that he has lost, I know that he needs to do this. I waited for him in the bedroom. At first, I felt silly trying to be sexy with my belly and swollen feet, feeling more like a blimp than the cheeky pixie who caught his eye years ago. Then I remember that Orion has always made me feel precious. From the moment he found me at Hanna's home he has shown me how beautiful he thinks I am. He is constantly kissing my belly and having chats with Gabriella. When he is done, he tells her to fall asleep so he can play with mommy. He takes his time worshipping my body. Always so gently and lovingly. And although I can't complain about the ability to come every time, I miss the fast, hard sex. Orion is worried it'll hurt me or the baby and after having had a rough start to the pregnancy, he doesn't want to lose control. I miss that. I miss him losing control and thrusting hard inside me until we both scream in delight.

I was going to blow his mind. I reclined on the bed, arranging the pillows to make myself more comfortable with less pressure on my back. Orion has always loved my legs. I may only be five-foot-three and a half—I tell everyone five-foot-four—but my legs are toned. When he runs his hands up and down my legs, my insides tingle. I casually draped one leg over the other allowing the lace hem to lift, showing the matching panties. I only left the lamp on the far table on, softening the lighting. I set candles on either side of the bed. I made sure to wear Orion's favorite scent. I strategically dabbed the perfume behind my ears, collarbone and behind my knees.

Orion stood at the doorway and takes in the scene I have set. I saw his torso flex, his jaw tightened, and his eyes illuminated. He liked it. My heart fluttered. He strutted over to me, yanking off his Satan's Pride vest and tossing it on the nearest chair. He grabbed the hem of his tee, tearing his off, revealing his glorious, massive chest. He is a big man; his chest and shoulders are wide, firm and fit. His arms are huge, clearly indicating how much he works at maintaining his body. I followed the path to the magnificent vee. I itched to release his belt buckle. Anticipating my thoughts, Orion came to stand above me, forcing my head back to look into his face. He aligned me so that I am fully on my back and he was straddling my legs with his hands fisted on other side of my head.

"Pretty girl, you're playing with fire," he whispered a hair's breadth away from my mouth. I licked my lips.

"I want fire." I was already wet. Just the way he carried himself into the room, his strength; it blows my mind and I am a puddle. I remembered that this night is for Orion and pull myself together.

"We discussed this, baby. We need to go soft until the baby is born. Then I promise you, as soon as we get the go ahead from the doctor, I am going to fuck you against the wall. Just like the first time we ever fucked. I am going to rip off your panties, lift you off the ground, back you into the wall and fuck you so hard that you aren't going to be able to walk for a week. Every time you move, you will remember that moment," he whispered seductively. I was panting. I wanted that so badly. My eyes were wide, and he knows that nothing makes me hotter than taking him deep and hard. "Until then baby, I need to go slow and steady. I always get you there, baby, don't I?" he asked.

"Always," I said and ran my fingers up from his deep vee to his broad shoulders. "Let me love you tonight. I want to make love to you," I said beseechingly as I licked his chest and took a nip at his skin.

"You going to do me soft and slow?" he asked, and I could feel his massive cock through his jeans poking into my thigh.

"Uh huh." I continued to pepper his chest with nips and kisses.

He slid off the bed and removed his jeans and boxers. He is impressive. It doesn't matter how often I see him like this, I want him desperately. He maneuvered onto the bed and I placed my hands on his chest to direct him onto his back. I licked his lips and kissed him deeply. He immediately held my head in place and ran his fingers through my hair. He didn't release me until we were both breathless. "Perfect for me, Vi," he said quietly. My eyes shone with emotion.

"I want to show you how much you mean to me," I said.

"Have at it, baby," he replied. He dropped his hands and winked at me. He placed his hands behind his head.

I caressed his chest, making my way lower. I kissed each hip bone and lick downward until I reached his cock. I ran my hands gently over his scrotum and massaged softly. Then caressed his thighs. He rearranged the pillows. He was propping himself up to get a better view of the festivities. I pushed his legs apart and he quickly acquiesced as I adjusted myself to sit on my haunches between his legs. I kissed his right thigh and continued all the way up, stopping right before I got to the main course, then began again with his left, all the while massaging his sensitive areas. His stomach contracted and he groaned loudly and growled with every touch as I grew closer to his cock.

"You keep teasing me, woman, and I am going to take over," he warned.

"Patience, Bear," I told him. And as he was about to respond. I licked up the length of him, hearing him hiss in response. I lavished his cock with long slow licks, flicking the tip. He was so sensitive, and I intended to intensify that feeling. I dipped my tongue into the slit and teased it. I rolled my tongue around and around the tip until I closed my lips over the tip and sucked gently. His hands clenched the sheets and he was staring into my eyes as I sucked his cock.

"Fuck, pretty girl," he moaned.

I took him deeper into my mouth and continued to suck. I bobbed my head and took him as deep as I could and used my hands to continue stroking him. The muscles in his legs tensed and his abs were clenched.

"Baby," he warned.

I pulled back with a pop. Orion watched as I climbed over his thighs and positioned myself just above his member. I pulled my panties to the side, holding them with one hand, the other guided him inside me. I slid down, taking him deep. All the way down until I felt all of him. He felt too good and I moaned with need, reveled in the moment.

"Vi, baby, you gotta move," Orion said through clenched teeth. His jaw was taunt, and he was showing supreme strength in keeping control. He had let me lead him and I wanted to make sure he felt my love for him. I took his hands and placed one on my breast and with the other, I took his finger together with mine and rubbed it gently over my clit. Immediately my pussy clenched, tightening around him. "Fuck," he growled.

I lifted myself up and down over him, taking him in and clenching hard around him as he continued to strum his fingers over my clit. I began to lose control, going faster and harder when Orion navigated into a sitting position and held my hips steady as he pushed himself up into me. He was relentless in his endeavor to find our euphoria. "Get there, baby," he moaned.

"Together," I panted.

"Now, baby," he replied. I clenched him tight and felt him fill me up. I heard his roar mixed with mewls from a cataclysmic orgasm.

I couldn't move. He lifted me off him and laid me beside him so that we were facing each other. He pulled my leg over his and stroked my warm, damp cheek, our foreheads touching.

"Thank you for loving me, Vi. I never thought I would feel this again."

So now, it's so important that Nate like me. I want my man to have everything.

CHAPTER 18

Bratty Brother

Orion

It's good to be back at Molly's. Vi is greeted at the door by Molly and refuses to release her for a good ten minutes. Vi was worried about seeing her. She was upset that she hurt Molly badly and would not be welcomed back. That was never going to happen. First off, she is Vi and anyone who knows her knows that she would never leave like she did without good reason. Secondly, I am a Satan's Pride member, and no one disrespects my woman, brothers, or club.

The regulars all drop by our table to give Vi a hug and tell her how glad they are that she's back. Vi instantly perks up and begins being her gabby self, smoothing over any ripples that may have been caused by her absence with her brilliant smile. Vi was sipping coffee and waving to Hanna who had come in the back to drop of the weekly order placed by Molly. It's then that the overhead bell tinkles to indicate someone is walking in.

Nate treks inside wearing his traditional business suit. I'm sure it cost a mint. Nate always loved the good stuff. He spots me immediately and makes his way over. I stand to greet him and that gets Vi's attention. He takes my hand and pulls me in for a brotherly hug, slapping my back for good measure.

"Hey big brother," Nate says. I pull back and help Vi to stand. Nate is almost as tall as me, but has a slimmer build. I get my hair cut when I remember, and Nate has a standing appointment every two weeks. Despite all that has happened between us, we remain close, or as close as our dad would allow.

"Yo Nate," I greet him. "I want you to meet Vi." Vi shyly stretches out her hand to say hello and Nate looks at her hand and takes it in his, pulling her into a hug. That's my brother. Family is family.

"Hi Nate, it's really nice to meet you finally," Vi says.

"Same here, Vi." Nate replies. "Let's take a seat. It looks like you need to be off your feet." He assists her into a chair and asks, "How much longer before I meet my niece?"

"Just a little longer to go. I can't wait for Gabriella to show her face and I can see my toes again," Vi laughs.

"Then we don't sleep," I remind her with a grin.

"I don't sleep now. I think she has taken up kickboxing in there and is using my bladder as the punching bag," Vi whines.

BRATTY BROTHER

"Sorry, pretty girl, just a little longer," I sympathize.

"Shit, it's amazing to see you two doing this," Nate says and floats his hand between us. He turns his attention to me. "It's good to see you so happy, Gavin." It's authentic. "Tell me about yourself, Vi. Gavin tends to leave shit out."

Vi chats about her business, our new home, her friends Ava, Maddie, and Hanna, who has become an unofficial Lady Pride. Not even Hanna knows it yet, although Ava and Maddie agree. She asks Nate about his business, his wife Emily. They are behaving as if they have known each other their whole lives. Completely comfortable with one another. I interject from time to time, but my focus is to include Vi in all areas of my life. No hidden secrets.

"So, Gavin, I have to ask, any way we can get you and Dad to talk things out and really be a family?" Nate inquires.

"Nate…" I start.

"Listen for just a minute," he interrupts. "Dad doesn't even know that he is going to have a grandchild. The man should know. It may make him more receptive to talking and burying the past."

"Nate, I love you from the bottom of my soul. He is your dad. To me, he was just a man who impregnated my mother. You know what we lived through. You know how he reacted to my choices. Do you really think I want a man like that around my kid?" I lay out.

"He's getting older, Gavin. This may change him," Nate says optimistically.

"He misses his big brother, honey," Vi teases to lighten the mood.

Nate quips right back. "I was beginning to like you, Vi."

"You like me. I'm likeable," she responds. At that moment, Nate's phone chimes.

"It's Dad," he says. "I haven't checked in since my meeting. He's probably wondering why. I'll call him back in a bit."

"Don't bother," We hear from the front door. There he is in all his pompous glory—Ian Moore.

"Shit," says Nate.

"Oh my," says Vi, her eyes wide.

"Fuck," I add.

"That's a greeting," says dear old Dad. "I see that my two sons are consorting behind my back."

"We are not consorting, Dad. I just wanted to see Gavin and his girlfriend, Vi," Nate answers.

"What is wrong with you, Nathan? Gavin walked out on us years ago and here you are, begging for his attention? That's just sad," he belts out, in front of all the patrons in Molly's.

Ian whips his head over to me. "I see you got another one pregnant. You just can't keep it in your pants, can you?" He looks Vi over, than announces, "I don't care what you were told but unless I see a paternity test, I will not be changing my will."

Vi's head snaps back at the insult. A gasp come out of her sweet lips.

"You've said enough, asshole. Father or not, you are not welcome here." Guard must have come in during the verbal blows and has heard enough. He is fuming. I've seen Guard angry and it is not a good look. "No one talks about Vi that way and no one insults my brother. Get the fuck out!"

BRATTY BROTHER

"With pleasure," Ian spits out.

"Wait," says Vi. She takes a couple of steps forward towards Dad and I instinctively move to stop her when Nate holds me back.

"You are a very sad man. I pity you. You have missed out on precious time with your son. He is smart, sweet, gentle, generous and he knows what is important in life. They call him Orion. Do you know why?" she continues without hesitation. "Orion is a hunter. His brothers know they can rely on him to get the job done. I am never fearful when he is by my side. This town respects him. His brother comes to see him in hiding so that they can be together. The problem here is not my man, the problem is an old man who is too stubborn to say he's sorry and move forward."

Vi moves closer. "If you do not stop this war that you began and bury the past, you will never see your granddaughter. You will never feel the peace and goodness of family and for that, I pity you." The she places the final nail in the coffin. "I never knew my father; he was weak and pathetic and left before I was born, but right now, I am happier to have had him for a father than you."

With that, she steps back and runs into my arms. "I'm so sorry you lived with that, honey. He doesn't deserve all the greatness that is you."

"Shh, babe. He is gone. Out of our lives." I hold her tight.

I look at my father. "You and I are done. I don't care if you insult me, I've heard it my entire life. But no one touches Vi or my baby girl. Don't ever come back here."

"Let's go Nathan," he calls out.

"Hell no!" Nate explodes. "I am not your dog. You don't follow me here to make a scene and ruin my precious time with my brother. You do not insult Vi and think that's okay. Go home. I need to calm down. And Dad, you may need to look for someone to take over my position. This is the final straw."

"You'll be back, Nathan. You need me," Dad says and walks out the door.

"I can't believe he tracked the GPS on my phone. I argued with him the last time he did this shit and he promised to let it go. He agreed that he needed to trust me and then he goes and pulls shit like this. I'm so sorry Vi, you certainly didn't deserve to see that. Orion, brother, I had no clue he was onto me.", Nate apologized.

Guard follows him out to ensure that he is in his car and leaving. Nate sits in his chair with his hands holding his head. I sit Vi back down. I am doing my best to not follow him and beat the shit of the man who is supposed to be my father. I am so close to storming out of the shop and hunting him down.

"Baby, no." I hear Vi, as she reaches out to grab my hand. "Sit with us. Nate and I need you. Let him go. He doesn't deserve your time or thoughts."

I wrestle with the options and come to see that the past walked out the door. Vi is my future.

"Shit, I just quit my job," Nate says, and then starts laughing.

"I'm sure he will take you back," Vi says.

"Not going back," he says between laughter.

"What are you going to do, Nate?" I ask.

'Don't know yet. I am going to talk to Emily. She is going to be happy. She was having a hard time

BRATTY BROTHER

being civil to the old man. She has wanted me to start my own business for a long time. Maybe, now's the time," Nate says.

Guard reenters with Risk by his side and joins our table. "You alright?"

"Yeah", I say.

Hanna walks over with a tray of goodies. Placing a small dessert dish before each of us. "Vi, lemon square, an extra big piece. Orion, Éclair bites, three because the situations calls for it. Guard, an extra-large piece of chocolate hazelnut pie. Nate, I don't know you, but you strike me as a cinnamon kind of guy. Cinnamon rolls with walnuts. And Risk, here is your favorite key lime pie with almond crust." She walks away without saying another thing.

Vi grabs a fork and digs into her dessert. "So, tell me Nate, were you the typical bratty brother?" she asks as she inhales her first bite.

The table erupted with laughter. Although I catch Risk watching Hanna walk away while chuckling with the rest of us.

CHAPTER 19

The chair

Vi

Our home is ready. Orion and his crew have been putting up curtain rods and curtains. The appliances have been delivered and Risk in in the kitchen with Orion, getting the final installations complete. We purchased a slew of new furniture, seeing as I didn't have any and Orion wanted to leave his stuff at the compound so that if we decide to stay the night, we'd still have a bed there. Guard is putting together the kitchen with War and then all of them are going to complete the bedroom. Ava and Maddie had been helping me put together the kitchen until we were told to take a break, giving the men room to get their stuff done.

On Orion's request, I sit myself down on the midnight blue, tufted high back chair with my feet resting on the matching ottoman. Maddie passes me a glass of iced tea and then bends to talk to the baby. "Hey, baby girl, Auntie Maddie is working on a song just for you. I will have it ready for the day you arrive in this world," she says. Suddenly a little hand bumps at my belly, indicating she is excited to hear Auntie Maddie sing to her.

"She hears you, Maddie." I laugh at Maddie's expression of surprise.

"I hope that she and Gavin become best friends," Ava says. "I have Cris looking after him today. He gets cranky when he misses his afternoon nap."

"They better get along; we are always together," I tell them.

"I bet Cris is great with him. He is so calm, and I bet that Gavin is just loving all the attention." Maddie refills the cookie plate and holds it out for me to grab a couple. Lately, I have been grabbing cookies to supplement my lemon bar deprivation.

"Heading to the bedroom, Vi," Orion announces as he walks through with the guys. Orion has settled in. He is much calmer and is constantly sharing information. After the debacle with Nate and his dad, I wasn't sure how it would affect him.

Orion and the club have decided to invest in Nate's new business venture. Guard ran it through the club members, and they all agreed it was a sound plan. Nate shared his vision and business plan with the crew. Orion will be contracting the IT portion so they will have the best security system possible. We all got to meet Emily, Nate's wife. She is adorable. Tall and blonde with pretty blue eyes. She was poised and open. Ava and Maddie liked her instantly and I was so

THE CHAIR

thrilled that she wanted to bridge the gap between Nate and Orion. I want my baby girl to have all her aunts and uncles in her life. Ian has made no contact with Nathan or Orion since the incident at the diner. The guys seem fine with it, but I am not. I want my baby girl to have grandparents as well.

"Vi!" Orion's roar booms through the house. It shakes me and I almost dropped my cookie. I push myself up and out of the chair and waddle down the hall, cookie still in hand.

"What? You almost made me drop my cookie." I pout as I walk through the doorway.

"That chair goes," Orion says. His hand points to the blue chair that Maddie purchased for me almost a year ago. I love that chair. Maddie bought it just for me. It's so comfortable, I can't wait to snuggle in it with my baby.

"I love that chair," I say, taking a bit of my cookie.

"It goes," he commands.

"It stays," I insist.

"It goes and that's the end of it." Orion starts to walk toward the chair to pick it up. I am not sure if it's the hormones or his tone that sets me off, but I lose it!

"Now see here, that chair is a gift from my friend. Maddie chose it for me. And it stays," I yell. That's right, I yell at a giant. His face is menacing. He is ticked. I mean really, really mad.

The men exit the room, leaving the two of us having a staring contest. Orion begins to stalk out after them when I grab his arm.

"Oh, no you don't. We are not going to go back to not speaking about what is going on between us." I force the subject. "It's just a chair. Why are you so mad?" I ask, confused by his reaction.

"Do you know what that chair reminds me of?" he spews. "It reminds me that I wasn't there to protect you. I fell short. You almost died and I didn't do my job keeping you safe. You were beaten to a bloody pulp and I had to see you bloody. When they were done at the hospital, most of your body was bandaged and that, right there, is where you sat," he points to the chair. "I had to see you aching and I saw you hold in the tears whenever you moved. The chair is where you sat through your recovery. I hate that chair." Orion is pacing around the room trying to control himself after the outburst.

I stare in stunned silence. I know he was affected by the violence I suffered. I had no idea how much he blamed himself. I walk over and wrap my arms around his waist, as far as they will go with my belly taking up so much space.

"I'm sorry for being insensitive. I had no idea that's how you felt. I saw this as a beautiful gift from a friend. This is the place where you held me in your arms while I healed. Those are the moments I remember. I don't want to fight over this and we can get rid of it, but I want to you to really think about it " I want to keep the chair but there is no way it is more important than the hurt it is causing Orion. I don't want a chair to have this effect on him. I try a different approach.

"Orion, this chair reminds you of me hurt being. This chair reminds me of how gentle you were carrying me and placing me in it. I remember you sitting in it with me, settling me on your lap and letting

THE CHAIR

me sleep, leaning into you, because it was the most comfortable position for me at the time. I sit in this chair and I see the two of us together. I recall the warmth and peace. I want to give that to our daughter. I want to take a picture of you holding me and me holding her. All three of us snuggled together. But if you can't see that then we need to let it go because you mean more to me than a chair." I want Orion to know that this object is just an object.

His arms wrap around me. "Keep it."

"Not if you can't get past it," I state.

"I need to get used to seeing it in here."

"We can start by sitting in it together. I am not bandaged or hurting, and neither are you." I say.

"Tonight, after we get this room built," he blows out a breath.

"Kay." I turn to leave the room.

"Can you send the guys back here?" he says, "I want to start making new memories."

I give him a small smile. He quirks his lip upward. Crisis averted. My man's okay, so I'm okay.

CHAPTER 20

Orion will come

Vi

The last few weeks have been a dream. A wonderful dream. Mom and Aaron have come for a visit and although Orion is not thrilled with the way they treated me in the past, he understands that we are all moving forward. Mom is still recovering physically but emotionally seems better. She has been respectful about her time with us and I have been upfront with the hurt I have felt and that we need to start off small. Aaron has doted on mom and has shown his loyalty to her time and time again. That was never the issue. I can see that he is trying very hard to make an effort with both Orion and me. Orion is not as forgiving and is making him work for it. I must say I am surprised to see him sucking it up and doing what he can. They brought gifts for Gabriella. Apparently, Mom is very crafty and had created a photo album. The book has baby lambs on the cover and each page fits a picture and beneath it, a place to script the most important moments as our baby grows.

Nate and Emily have been in touch as well. Orion and Nate have been working together on how to move forward businesswise and they are spending more time reconnecting. Risk has been by often. He is happy for Orion. They stood side-by-side when they were in Special Ops and they stand together now. Feels good to know that he has Orion's back. Guard and Ava have been wonderful too, dropping by to share Gavin with us, letting Orion revel in getting to know his namesake. Another regret that Orion had in not becoming attached to the little fellow. Little Gavin is a character and I can see that he is going to give Guard grey hair. Maddie has been on the road with War for a few shows but they are back now. I see how they took a complicated situation and came through the other side more in love.

Cris is my bodyguard today. Orion is constantly worried about leaving me alone in our home when I am due soon. I love that Cris and Demon can speak to each other without actually talking. Both are loyal members and will become full-fledged members of Satan's Pride within the next month. They deserve it. Loyal, devoted, true.

Orion is meeting a close friend from another chapter of Satan's Pride. Saint and he have spoken often since Orion and I have been together, but I have never met him. Orion says he is a true brother and he must be if he is in another chapter and he is taking the time to meet up. Hence why Cris is stuck with me all day. Poor boy.

I have been working in my workroom. Orion surprised me with a special space for my business when Risk designed our new place. He transferred everything from Hanna's place and had proper shelving, cabinets, and a computer desk put in. He kept the walls cream and placed a girly chandelier in the room. The rest is up to me to me to decorate as I see fit. I haven't gotten to that yet, but I have time.

I haven't seen Hanna for a couple of weeks. I am definitely craving a lemon square and her sweetness. I miss our chats. I am sure it will be an easy task to get Cris to come with me to pick up some dessert. He has a huge sweet tooth.

I see Cris on the couch, watching the news. I raise my hands palm up and shrug my shoulders.

"Lemon square?" I say simply.

A wide toothy grin appears on his face. Yes! I knew he'd be in. He stands and walks to the door, waving his hand for me to follow him out the front door.

As we park in front of the shop, Cris's phone rings.

"Hey," he answers. "I'm with Vi, in front of Hanna's." There is a quick pause before he continues. "Right, I need to see Vi in first and check the place out."

I hear murmurs on the other end of the phone. Cris then asks me, "You good with staying put for a half hour while I pick up Gavin and Ava and bring them here?"

"Awesome. The more the merrier," I say happily. True to his word, Cris takes me in and does a walk through. There are two other patrons in the shop and of course, Hanna. She is wearing a pale-yellow t-shirt and loose-fitting jeans. Her face is clean of makeup and her hair up in a messy bun. She smiles cheerfully and hands a snicker-doodle cookie to Cris before he walks out to pick up Ava.

I hug Hanna tightly. "I have missed you, Hanna. You haven't been to visit for a while. I want you to come and see our new place."

"I thought I'd give you and Orion some time to get situated before coming by. I don't want to intrude. You've often got so many friends coming and going, I thought you could use some time to yourselves," Hanna replies.

"Hanna, you are my family. Orion cares about you too. Please come by," I tell her.

"Okay, sweetie. I will. I've missed our chats," she says shyly.

I take a seat at the table closest to the counter. "Ooh, just so you know, Ava and Gavin will be here soon," I announce.

"I love that little guy. He is so sweet. I love his snuggles," she replies as she moves to grab a dish for my dessert. The bell above the door dings.

"Thanks, Hanna. Later Vi!" call out Alana and Miles. They are a sweet, young couple. First loves are super cute.

Hanna turns back to her task of getting my lemon bar and lemon ginger tea, when a man comes in as the young couple are leaving. I haven't seen him in town before. He has straight brown hair and inset eyes. He's average height, definitely not taller than Orion, but way taller than me. Then again most everyone is taller than me. He seems distracted and is looking anxiously around the shop. What he does next lets me know we are in trouble.

This stranger locks the shop door. Then turns back to me. "Where is Hanna?" he asks snidely, obviously too high to see her crouched down behind the counter.

I sense rather than see the tension ricocheting off Hanna behind the counter. She knows him. She's frightened of this man.

"Well," I start.

"Before you start with the lies," he says and pulls a gun out of this jacket pocket, "this is the time to rethink your answer."

I shudder at the sight of the gun in his hand. The memories of Jeffery's attack, of the gun he had pointed at me while he beat me to get information, flood my mind. Does this happen twice? My hand drops to my belly.

"Please, I am pregnant," I tell him, although this is something he can see for himself.

"Not after you. I want Hanna." He hand is shaking, and I am terrified the gun is going to go off. Hanna stands up straight.

"Allan, I'm here," she says quietly. He immediately turns the gun towards Hanna. "Why don't we let Vi leave, then we can talk."

"You think I'm stupid. She's gonna call that fucking guy she's with," he spews. "She stays until you get in the car with me."

Hanna works her way to me. "I'm going to go

with Allan. You will be safe, Vi." Hanna grabs my trembling hand. If she gets into his car, she is going to be in huge trouble. My eyes go back to Allan and I know he is going to hurt her. He is twitching and when I look closer, I can see his eyes are glazed over. He is on something. High as a kite.

"Please don't do this." I shake my head pleadingly. "Hanna is such a good person."

He whips his head to Hanna, then back to me. With sheer disgust in his tone he says, "Saint Hanna. Always looking out for everyone, except her fucking husband. Right Hanna?!" He stalks towards us, the gun waving about. "Baking cookies for the neighbours, volunteering for food drives, always devoting her time to her fucking family. Everyone but me!" he screams in Hanna's face.

Hanna pulls me back a step, placing her body between Allan and me. Just then, my cell phone goes off where I dropped it on the table. The ringing is agitating Allan. He is staring fiercely at the phone, waiting for it to stop. The instant it stops, it begins again.

"It's probably my guy," I say. "If I don't get that, he will come barreling in here. Let me answer. Please." An idea comes to mind as I am saying the words.

"Get it. I have a gun pointed to your friend, so don't think of tipping him off," he says menacingly. He pushes the phone across the table towards me.

I pick it up with trembling fingers. Taking a breath, I answer. "Hi, honey. How are you?" I try and sound normal with the gun flitting back and forth between Hanna and me.

A gruff voice on the other side of the line replies, "Real good, pretty girl. I am close to home. See you in a few."

"I'm at the bakery honey. I was having a craving for my favorite strawberry tarts and I was going to bring home peanut butter balls for you. I know how much you love them," I try to sound as casual as possible. My eyes go to Allan for fear that he has caught on, but his focus is on Hanna.

"Right, baby, you better bring plenty back because I brought Saint home to meet you," he says. "Who is picking you up?"

"Hopefully Cris will be around soon," I say. Allan takes that moment to pull Hanna away and wrap an arm around her waist, pointing the gun to her head. He mouths the words, *hang up*.

"Got to go, honey. Hanna needs me to grab a tray for her in the kitchen," I lie. I hang up without waiting for a response.

"Good girl, Vi," Allan sneers. "Now I gotta take my wife home to teach her a lesson." He bends so that his mouth is at her ear. "Gonna take you home and fuck you bloody. A bad wife needs to be taught a lesson." I see the tears building in Hanna's eyes, but she stays silent. He wraps a hand around her throat and squeezes. I can hear Hanna gasp for breath. I rush to help her and am stopped in my tracks when he points the gun at my belly.

He lets go of Hanna's throat and a gasp escapes her lips. She is struggling for air. "Don't worry, Hanna. I'll save the fun stuff for when we are alone." He laughs and hauls Hanna towards the door. "Unlock it," he commands. She reaches out to flip the lock. He backs himself through the door, dragging Hanna along with him. I race to the door when I hear a crash and then the pop of the gun going off. I hate the sound. My hands cover my mouth while I scream in shock.

I fall to my knees. The door is wretched open, and Orion is racing through the door. His right arm is holding his left. When I look closer, I see blood and begin to shake like a leaf.

"Baby," I whisper reaching for him. He kneels before me, wrapping his good arm around my shoulders.

Running in after Orion is a beast of a man I haven't met. He has Allan by the throat and tosses him to the floor across from us. Risk is carrying Hanna into the shop. She is unconscious and limp in his arms. There is a flurry of activity and I hear Risk on the phone. A short while later, Guard and War rush in along with Sherriff James.

Guard comes to us immediately and helps me up, while War is assisting Orion. I turn my head in confusion to see Allan in cuffs and Risk sitting in a chair while the man I believe to be Saint is checking her pulse. His voice is calm, "Risk, she needs to be checked out at the hospital. Her vitals are good, but we aren't taking any chances." He turns to Orion. "Gotta check the wound, bud."

"It's just a flesh wound," Orion retorts.

"Ambulance is on its way and you're going," this man says sternly.

That's when it happened. A flood of water rushes between my legs. It's all too much. My head begins to spin, and I feel myself drop. Two arms catch me mid-fall.

"VI!" I hear Orion call.

"You found me, grizzly," I slur, then darkness takes me.

CHAPTER 21

Gabriella's Arrival

"I need to get to Vi," I tell the nurse. The older woman looks at me sympathetically. The doctor in the emergency room stitched me up after checking that the wound was clear and just as I thought, it's just a superficial wound. The nurse is just finishing up. War is sitting in the chair, making sure I don't bolt to see Vi. Guard is with her.

I left Vi in a gurney being wheeled into a room. She regained consciousness in the ambulance. The paramedics treated her for shock and quickly put her on oxygen. Within a few minutes she was looking around the back of the ambulance for me. I took her hand with my good one. Hanna was taken in a second ambulance and Risk rode with her.

She was stable when I was separated from her. I would not have left her side if not for her words. "Baby, I need to know you are going to be okay. Please go with the nurse, get taken care of and come back to me as soon as you can." She squeezed my fingers and, in that moment, she had her first major contraction. "Hurry," she gritted through her teeth.

Hanna's ex-husband is sitting in a cell. He should be in a morgue. He would be if the Sherriff didn't show up. Risk had him on the ground, his fist hitting his face repeatedly. War threw him off before he killed him. Risk took one look at Hanna being strangled against her car with a gun pointed at her head and tore at him like a bull. Allan turned the gun on Risk. I tackled him just in time to cover and dive to the pavement with Risk. Unfortunately, the bullet nicked my upper arm. The blood made it look much worse that it was. When I looked up, I saw War had Allan subdued, and tore into the bakery to see Vi. I found her on her knees. Saint was running from the street, followed closely by the Sherriff.

Tears were streaming down her face. She took one look at me and then at Hanna being carried in by Risk and I knew that she was reliving the tragedy that happened to her. Guard and War came to help us stand. We steadied Vi on her feet and suddenly a gush of water splashed onto the floor. In that moment, Vi passed out. I panicked. Guard caught her, making sure she never hit the ground.

Now I am itching to get to her. I am finally released and race down the corridor to the elevator toward the neonatal ward. War is a step behind me. I step off the elevator to see Saint, Ava, Maddie, even

GABRIELLA'S ARRIVAL

little Gavin and the rest of my brothers filling the waiting room.

"Where's Vi?" I ask as I approach the crowd.

"Her room is that one and Guard hasn't left her side," Ava says, smiling at me.

I nod and walk past the crew to Vi. She's in bed, holding on tight to Guard's hand and breathing deeply. "I got this," I tell Guard and step in beside the bed to take my place. "Thanks, man."

"Told you before, brother, we got your back. And Vi's. Called Nate and he and Emily are driving in," he informs me.

The doctor and nurse walk in as Guard makes his exit. "Let's check to see if we're ready to have this bundle," says the doctor. After a quick check, she affirms that it's go time.

"Thank you for coming to me, my grizzly bear. I was praying that you caught my clue." She grits her teeth as another contraction hits her.

"My pretty girl loves her lemon bars. Strawberry tarts have never been your thing," I tease. "Everyone knows that Peanut Butter Balls are Cris's thing. I called him as soon as I hung up with you to keep Ava and Gavin safe." I kiss her gently. "My brave beauty."

Vi is a champ. The contractions are strong, and she is pushing as the doctor orders. I stand behind her and push her forward to help her push as shown by the nurse. I offer Vi words of encouragement, telling her how proud I am, how much she means to me. I kiss her forehead. My brave Vi. She is so tired and in so much pain. "Isn't there anything you can give her?" I ask with a great deal of worry.

"Not at this point. Anyway, Vi has insisted on a

natural birth when we first started talking about this, don't you remember. She is doing great," the doctor says. "The baby is crowning. You're almost there, Vi. A couple bigger pushes and you get to see you precious miracle," she encourages.

I move to Vi's side. "Pretty girl, you can do this. I'm here, baby."

"Kay," she says, panting. A hard push and I can see the baby coming. I am in awe of the strength and resilience of my woman. Beautiful to the core.

"Welcome to the world, Baby Girl Moore." The nurse says happily, placing Gabriella on Vi's chest. The baby's cries quiet and Vi covers her body with her hand while still holds mine with the other. I bend to kiss Vi soundly on the mouth, then turn my attention to Gabriella and place a soft kiss on her head. I will let the others know in a little while. I want this time with my future wife and baby.

CHAPTER 22

Guard/Gabriella

Orion

The entire Pride crew is in the waiting room an hour later. I notice my brother, Nate, running into the room with his wife.

"Am I in time?" Nate pants. It's obvious that he and Emily were running through the hospital to get to us.

"Well?" asks Emily.

I am smiling like an idiot. "Gabriella Olivia Moore wants to say hello to each and every one of you. They are settling Vi with Gabi and she is doing amazing. She wants me to make sure each and every one of you know that you being here confirms that this is home. I know it means a lot for Vi to see you all, so I am going to ask you all to settle in for a while until they allow you to see her." I see Ava and Maddie sniffling, holding back tears of happiness. Ava clings to Guard with Gavin in his arms. Maddie is wrapped tight into War, looking up at him with joy. Emily is hanging on to Nate's arm and my brother gives me a look that only we understand. We made it. Despite the chaos of our childhood, we made it.

Demon, Cris, and Saint are all here as well. I see Risk is missing. Guard reads my mind. "Risk is staying with Hanna until her family get here. He has been back and forth the whole time."

I nod. Seems to me that Risk is taking a vested interest our little baker. I smirk at the thought. Guard catches my lip quirk. He nods and smiles as well.

"Can we see her?" Ava questions.

"Absolutely. She wants to see you all. I was thinking that we can let Ava, Maddie and Emily go first. Then she wants to see you Guard, Nate and War and so on," I tell them.

Ava is quick to smack a kiss on Guard's cheek and runs through the double doors that lead to Vi's room. Maddie and Emily are quick on her trail. The guys take one look at the women in the throes of babyhood and burst out laughing. I am surrounded by my brothers, all wishing me congratulations, patting my back and shaking my hand.

After delivering the news and getting everyone caught up, I ask them to stand watch over my family. It's time to go see Hanna. She led me back to Vi and there is nothing I wouldn't do for her. The idea of that shitface suffocating her and slamming her against the car tears at me. If he makes it out of prison, he won't be breathing for long. This I vow. Both he and

GUARD/GABRIELLA

Maddie's stalker have not yet begun to pay for the evil they produced.

I arrive at Hanna's room and see Risk in the chair beside her bed, head in hands. Hanna appears to be asleep. The vicious marks across her neck are a reminder of the brutality she endured. Risk's head pops up at the sound of my steps. I know that look in his eyes. I see his guilt over not anticipating her ex's vile hate. I see his sadness. I walk over and place my hand on his shoulder.

"How did you get through it?" he utters with a tormented voice.

"Focus on her getting healthy. Can't change what happened but we can guide her through the pain and be there for her." I recall the nightmares that Vi had for the first month. She woke crying and I took her in my arms and held her until she calmed and fell back to sleep. "Vi had rough times, and even though I fucked up later, during her recovery, I made sure I was always available to her."

"Yeah," he replies, choking on the word.

"Can I have a minute with her?" I inquire. "Go have your moment with Gabi. She and Vi are waiting for you."

He stands and gives me a hug and a black slap. "Congrats, man. Is she beautiful like her mom?"

"Go take a look, brother. She's fucking perfect," I confirm. I am bursting with pride.

He saunters to the doorway, looking back at me. "Watch her until I get back."

"Nothing touches Hanna, Risk. She's important to me too," I comfort him.

I walk closer to the bed as the door closes. She

ORION

seems peaceful. She has scratch marks and her eyes and lips are swollen. Her head has a bandage, probably from being thrown around. I sit in the newly vacated chair. I notice her eyelids flutter. She slowly opens her eyes with a groan of pain. After a few moments, her eyes focus on me.

"Orion," she croaks.

I take her hand and stop her immediately. "No, Hanna. No talking. Let me talk and you just listen, yeah?" I don't wait for her to acknowledge. "Vi is really worried about you. She went into labour right afterwards." Hanna gasps and places her hand over her mouth. I appease her. "All's good. Baby Gabriella is doing amazing. She weighs in at six pounds seven ounces. Vi is great. She wanted to come down and see you, but they say it's too soon. Expect her here tomorrow and she will bring Gabi with her." A shy smile springs forward.

"I told you once, Hanna, you are part of our family now. Nothing hurts you again," I express and hold her hand.

Tears are streaming down her face. "Sorry," she croaks. She blames herself. I begin to tell her that's whacked when the door opens and a gang of men, women, and kids pile through. Her family has arrived and apparently, they don't follow the rules either, just like my brothers.

"Who are you?" One of the men asks.

"Name's Orion. Just making sure Hanna wasn't alone while you were on your way," I soothe them. "I will give you time alone. Just so you know, my man, Risk, will be back to check in on her soon."

An hour later

"She's beautiful, Vi." Guard soothes as he is rocking Gabriella in his arms.

"I have been very patient, Guard. I unconditionally named my baby after you because I trust Orion. Want to tell me why?" Vi inquires.

"Orion and I were at a grave site. He was visiting his wife and child. I was visiting my grandfather. We were both hurting. Together we found Satan's Pride. Together we stand reborn to fight and stand together after all the pain we've endured. I respect him and couldn't love him more if he were blood. I never wavered, except one night when an unhealthy reminder of my grandfather's death came to light. The night Orion and I avenged my grandfather's death. Naming my son after him is my way of letting him know." The story is beautiful, albeit lacking in detail. I assume that this is because it falls under the umbrella of club business and the club business does not reach our wives and children.

"Thank you, Guard. It seems that Orion feels the same," Vi's sweet voice says.

I look to him and he looks back. Protecting our families, Satan's Pride, wives, and children. We stand united for them.

CHAPTER 23

A Lifetime

Vi

It's been six weeks; we are settling in with Gabi at home. Orion has been a doting daddy. He changes diapers without complaint. He wakes during all the feedings, allowing me to stay in bed while he brings Gabriella to me, so that I can breastfeed. He perches behind me and keeps me company, then takes the baby and lulls her back to sleep in her basinet.

It's also been six sexless weeks! Watching my man holding his baby daughter, cupping her baby bootie, clad only in a diaper, nestled on daddy's muscular bare chest, makes me melt. His soft low cooing voice. So smooth and sexy.

One night I invited him to shower with me. Orion did not relent. He took me to our chair, that's right I said *our chair,* sat himself in it with placed me on his lap, then kissed me with passion until we were both out of breath and panting. Then he finally said, "Nothing hurts you, pretty girl, not even me. We wait until the doctor gives the all clear. You're worth the wait, baby. That kiss should tell you how much I want you, never doubt it."

Hells Bells! How do I argue with that?

But today, I got the all clear. I am jumping out of my car to let Orion know and praying that Gabriella is still napping. I reach the front door, with the intention of placing my key in the lock, when it is thrown open and I find Orion on the other side. He pulls me into the house, closing the front door behind me, then bracing me back against the door. The shock has left me winded. His eyes are glorious, smoldering. I know that look. He wants me. His body presses until I feel him along the length of my body. His cock is thick and straining against his jeans.

"Pretty girl?" I know what he needs to hear.

"First, how is little Gabi?" I ask.

"Naptime, baby."

It's a go." And I barely get the words out before my skirt is yanked up to my waist. I jump up, my legs automatically wrapping around his torso.

"Shirt."

I lift my top over my head and toss it over his shoulder. He takes a millisecond to reflect on the red lace bra I chose to wear for the occasion. I wanted to come home to my man ready.

"Tit."

I pull down the cup to expose my breast. Orion takes it in his mouth and laps gently. I am sensitive

A LIFETIME

there and an automatic jolt of electricity streams through my body. I expose the other one and he takes it into his mouth as he grinds his cock between my legs. I grow wetter and wetter. My hands find the messy curls at the back of his neck to pull him closer. I need this.

"Baby," I whisper. "More."

His lips lick the seam of mine, and he takes my lower lip and nips and sucks it. He pulls the gusset of my panties to the side with force.

"Look at me, pretty girl," he groans.

I stare into his eyes. With one full, forceful thrust he is inside me. My head drops back in sheer bliss.

"Eyes, baby." I drag my eyes back to him. "This is forever." And his slow sensual mesmerizing kiss makes my toes curl. Each stroke reaching me deep. He knows me, he knows my body. He hits my g-spot over and over. I am so close to the brink of ecstasy.

"Bear," I plead.

Orion plows into me harder. "Get there, baby." He roars.

He takes me over the edge of the mountainous cliff. I moan against his mouth, gripping his cock, holding him close, and fly.

Orion comes inside me a minute later, his mouth buried in my neck, his grunts and groans contained, to not wake our daughter. He is leaning against the door, careful not to place all his weight on me. I sift my hands through his hair, his head lifts and I kiss him softly. "You're right, baby. It was worth the wait."

"Not done yet, Vi." I have no idea how he still has the strength to carry me into our room and through to the bath, but he does. He sets me down and proceeds to undress me, kissing me thoroughly throughout the process. He turns on the water and when the steam is running hot, nudges me inside as he undresses. Then he joins me and washes my body with his large gentle hands. He massages shampoo into my hair and lathers me. I position myself under the water to rinse off and I turn so that my back is to his front.

He positions my hands on the tile in front of me. "Don't move them baby." I shiver in anticipation, a little tremor rolling through my entire being. His thick thigh comes between mine urging my legs further apart. I adjust my stance and feel his fingertips strum up and down my sides, his heavy breath at my ear. His hands stop right below the swell of my breasts, then he plucks and rolls them until I arch my back and let my head fall toward him, giving him better access. His mouth plants butterfly kisses along my jaw, shoulders, and the sweet spot on my neck. I take my hand off the wall to cup the back of his head, when a playful slap hits my ass cheek.

"Hands," is all he needs to say. Damn!

I demur and am rewarded when one hand snakes between my thighs where he plays with my pussy, his fingers strumming across the seam of my lips, then flitting over my clit seductively. I am ready for him again. My body moves to the rhythm of his fingers, itching for release. He positions his cock at my entrance and I take the tip of him. His hands move to cover mine on the wall. His front is molded to mine.

"You're mine, Vi," he whispers.

"For a lifetime," I reply.

"And beyond," he says and enters me fully. This time, he is slow, sensual. Torturously so. He hears my

A LIFETIME

frustration and drops his hand to my clit. I come immediately. I am overcome with my orgasm and as my breathing returns to normal, I hear his moan of release as well.

Our time is up, and Gabriella quickly reminds us of that with her sweet cry. Orion quickly rinses us off and wraps me in a towel. Kisses me softly and gets out of the shower to grab our girl.

He walks into our room as I am throwing on a short lilac robe. I'll dress after I feed her. He sits in our chair. "Come here baby."

"Got to feed our girl, Bear," I say as I walk over.

"In a minute." He sits me on his lap, while Gabriella is in the crook of his arm on the other. It's then that I notice a little box, laying open on Gabriella's swaddle. A beautiful ruby surrounded by tiny diamonds. I look at him, jaw dropped.

"You are my light and fire, Vivianna. You and my daughter and any other children we may have will own my heart. Marry me," he quietly commands in his bad boy biker way.

I place my forehead on his. "I love you too." He hands me Gabi while he takes the ring and slides it on to my finger. Our family for a lifetime.

CHAPTER 24

Cheap shot, Dad

Orion

The party last night was much tamer than most. I believed it was a good idea to have some time alone, just me and Vi. Demon was looking after Gavin and Gabi at our place. At first, we thought he was underestimating the task of taking on a toddler and a baby. But he insisted. We know Gabi is a good baby, but a toddler needs attention and Gavin is getting to the point where his curiosity is taking over. Guard has babyproofed his place and with the amount of time Ava and Gavin spend at ours, he has done the same to our house. Still, Demon said he had this and we agreed, mainly because we were at most, twenty minutes away from home. We when left, we heard Gavin babbling on, paying with blocks while Gabriella lay in her basinet, drifting off to sleep. Everyone knows that Demon is a man of very few words. It's rare that I get more than a syllable out of him, and yet I swear I heard him mumble in a low tone with Gavin, when he'd assumed we'd closed the door. I shut it quietly, not wanting to interrupt their interaction.

Maddie had returned from her last concert for a few months but she and War haven't been out of their place for a week. Every time War can't accompany Maddie, he is unbearable to be around. He takes security to a new level. Every man is screened by him, and he found a ex female navy seal to stay with her in the hotel suite to make sure that she is never feeling isolated or in danger. When she comes home, we get a call making us aware that calls will only be returned if they are urgent. I'm surprised that three days in, he has relented and agreed to come join us. I believe it was more Maddie who wanted to reconnect with her Pride sister, than anything.

Before the party was in full swing, the Satan's pride members congregated around the round table in our meeting room. When Saint first saw it, he said we were the Knights of the Roundtable. Most would say devils but that's because they don't get that we live and let live. What we don't do is allow anyone to tear apart what we've so carefully put together. Our businesses are solid. Our families are untouchable. Our brotherhood is loyal. Nothing, but nothing, breaks that.

Guard called the meeting to order. The first item on the agenda was Saint. He wants to shift his membership to our chapter. He is a full member in Chicago, spent over ten years with those men, but something is bringing him to us. I've known Saint since basic training. We served together. He had my back and I had his on more than one occasion. I know this man, so I know that Chicago is becoming a problem.

"Saint wants in. I have had a long conversation with him. I want him to give his reasons along with what he brings to the group. We decide together," Guard proclaimed.

Saint stood before us. "I served with a few of you. You know my character. I haven't changed. I want a life where brothers are just that brothers. The men in Chicago gave me that until Craze retired. They opted for a new Prez and I was cool with that. I didn't know him, but I figured that he had been part of the club for longer than me and saw no problem. After he took over, meetings started with the local mob scene. Drugs were becoming part of his protocol. Running them across the lines, I could live with. Running flesh, not good. I suspect he knew that I was not going to be good with it, so he hid it and none of the others told me. I only found out because a girl he was shipping was sick and they needed a medic. He would have let her die if she wasn't so important to him. Once I found out, I faked her death and found the means to transport her out of the country. Brink has no clue and after it happened, I told him I was out." He looked around the room, finally settling his eyes on me. "I save lives. I was a medic in the army. I am a doctor. I don't sell pussy or run drugs. I want to start a clinic in town and do what I am supposed to do. As far as I know, Brink doesn't give a shit if I leave. I have watched my back during my trip, and no one is after me. I wouldn't bring that shit to your doorstep. I will say that he is poising to strike. You are far enough that I don't think you're on his radar, but just a caution." He sits back down and waits.

"Right, you men heard his side. I have investigated along with Orion and Risk. Saint is right, this new Prez, Brink, is aiming to create a shit storm in his territory. We are keeping close watch, but no signs of transgressions have been made towards us as of yet." He turns to Saint. "We need to vote on it."

Around the room we went. Each man having his say. Yeses were heard all around. Demon, who still needed to vote regardless of being absent, gave his vote to Guard; in true Guard form, he slammed his hand down as Demon would have to give his assent. I can see Saint breathe a sigh of relief. He was homeless with a club. This has been his salvation after what he had been through and a nomad's life is never complete. Here he has a home.

The rest of the meeting was about our businesses, including the new startup with Nate. We have run into a few snags with dear old Dad. He is suing Nate and the company for soliciting his clientele. When Nate called me last week, he was beside himself with fury and worry. "I have money saved, Gavin, but I can't hold out until the end of a trial. I hate to tell you like this, but Emily is pregnant. I can't have her worrying." After I calmed him down, I called Guard with the warning that it was only a matter of time before we were served as well. Since the club is invested in the business, we decide together how to move forward. Unanimously, we decide to fight. Guard has researched the best lawyer, who will be around in the morning to have our first discussion. We agree that we

CHEAP SHOT, DAD

front for the lawyer and take it out of Nate's return on investment in installments, so that it doesn't cause him hardship. Nate has sent over every email of every current client, stating that they had already left the contract with Moore and would like to be quoted on a contract with N&S—us.

After the meeting ended, I called Nate. "Yo, Nate, how is Emily doing?"

"She's amazing. She is so excited, man. I love watching her pat her belly and talk to it," he said.

"Great, brother. More good news. We are fighting and we are not going to lose. Preliminary meeting is setup with our lawyer. She is topnotch. We are also taking care of the expenses. We will work out the payback later. For now, business as usual. Take care of Emily and come out for a visit, so Gabi can get to know Uncle Nate and Aunt Emily better," I told him.

A deep sigh and his tone is calmer. "Thanks, Gavin. So glad we're in this together."

"Me too," I replied.

Flash-forward to a night of Vi shaking her hips dancing and hearing her laughter with her family. It was an amazing evening. I knew Gabi was in good hands and we decided to head back and come back the next morning. That way Vi could pump her breast milk and give Demon a break. He insisted on bringing both Gavin and Gabi with him in the morning. We let him, after all, he would be right behind us.

The women are making breakfast, in the new kitchen Ava talks Guard into installing. The entertainment for the single men has left, either late last night or early this morning. We are about to sit down to coffee when the door chimes.

Cris tags the door and is barricading the entrance, so all we hear is a woman's voice. "I'm here for an appointed with Mr. Gabriel Stone and Mr. Gavin Moore. I am Sofia Donati."

"Follow me." Cris leads her in our direction.

Sofia Donati is a looker, I'll give her that. Wearing a tailored deep blue pencil skirt with a matching jacket and crisp white blouse, she carries a heavy briefcase. Sofia is the personification of professional. Heeled shoes, hair in a neat bun, even the chic glasses to top off her outfit. According to Guard, her skills are superior.

She stops just short of our table, scattered with coffee mugs and muffins. Sofia looks around the room with a polite smile. It's in this moment that Ava, Vi and Maddie walk out, carrying plates filled with scrambled eggs, bacon, toast, sausage, and hash browns. The ladies stop at the sight of Sofia.

"Hi," Vi says with a happy lilt to her voice. "Welcome. I'm Vi, and this is Ava and Maddie."

"Hello. It's a pleasure," Sofia replies kindly. Shifting her eyes to Guard. "If you are ready, we can go over my take on this problem. Then you can get back your gathering."

Ava pops in. "Join us."

"Thank you, I wish I could, but I have a lot to get back to the office. I have quite a lot to do." Her smile doesn't reach her eyes but is well-mannered. Saint chooses this exact moment to walk in wearing jeans with his shirt wide open . I see Sofia glance over and immediately returns her attention to Guard.

"Miss Donati, let me lead you to our office. Orion, you're with me." He walks over to Ava. "Make a plate for me, babe." He drops to kiss his wife. "Demon is coming with Gav and Gabi. We'll hang here for a while today."

Guard directs Sofia in the direction to the left of us and I follow behind them. Once seated, Sofia pulls out the documentation that has been accumulated by Nate and a private investigator that Guard hired. As soon as we heard from Nate, Guard went on the offensive.

"I see that you've been busy, Miss Donati. I hope you have good news for us," I say.

Sofia looks up from the paperwork she has spread across the desk. "Well, I have reviewed all the documentation. I see that Nate has been diligent in maintaining proper processes to negate the fact of soliciting clientele. Ian Moore does not have a leg to stand on in that regard. The issue is propriety property. Mr. Moore is stating that Nate and Gavin have procured and copied his firm's plans."

"That's ridiculous. Nate was the planner and the designs were his to start," I push back.

With a very cool look, she turns to me and states, "Mr. Moore, I understand your anger, however I did say this is his allegation, I did not say he would succeed in this endeavor. According to the law, while under the employ of a firm, the designs belong to the company. However, your brother is an extremely talented man and understood this, therefore he's made significant changes to his methods with full disclosure to every client to ensure they are aware of the changes and the benefits of those changes. Thus, allowing the decision to be an easy one."

Guard cuts to the chase. "Miss Donati, I understand your need to fully inform us of your findings. All I want to know is if he is going to drop the case."

"I'm afraid not. It seems that Ian Moore is seeking retribution. He is extremely irate at the loss of his prime designer and has taken to making this last as long as possible with the intention of crippling you financially. His lawyers have been instructed to find any excuse to delay proceedings. The only reason I know this is due to an immense favor owed to me by a colleague," she adds in frustration. "If this goes to court, you will undoubtably win, however, can you wait this out? I will be happy to negotiate my fee to assist you through this process, simply because I see the unfairness of it."

"Stop," Guard interrupts. "That won't be necessary Miss Donati. You have done extensive work and will be paid accordingly. I think that we have a key component that you may be missing."

Sofia quirks her eyebrow. "Please inform me, Mr. Stone."

"Ian Moore has been skimming the company. I have come into their financial data and have confirmed my findings. However, the clincher is this—Nathan and Gavin own half the company and he has never informed them. The late, Mrs. Moore, left her half of the company to be divided equally between her two sons."

"That is indeed a breach of ethics. How do you wish for me to proceed?" Sofia asks.

"Wait. What?" I yell. I turn to Guard. "How long have you known?"

"I got confirmation half an hour ago. I was going to tell you after breakfast."

CHEAP SHOT, DAD

"I want to talk to Nate," I tell them both. Guard nods and I pull out my phone to reiterate all that has gone down. After giving him the news, Nate is more upset than I. I see his point; he's been working for the asshole his whole life and he's kept him dangling on a string. He wants revenge. I agree. After hanging up, I turn to them both.

"Nate and I want our portion. So, if you want out, Guard, just say so. I get that this is a big move."

"Miss Donati, I believe you have your answer. Please make the call when you get to your office that we are moving forward and will be suing for half his company as stated in his mother's will," Guard announces.

"Am I assuming correctly in saying that you have the will in hand?" she asks. Guard pulls open the top drawer of his desk and yanks out a file. "Right here. I will have a copy scanned and emailed to you before noon."

"Excellent. I believe our business is concluded. Gentlemen, thank you for your time. I will be on my way and will make the call later today." Sofia is the epitome of precision.

We make our way back to the others. Saint is in a mood. He looks Sofia up and down. Sofia is not intimidated in the least. She doesn't flinch when he walks up to her and stops a short distance from her where she stands.

Sofia looks around at the table filled with Pride members. "It was nice meeting you." She turns to walk away, only to be stopped by Saint standing in her way. "Excuse me. I realize that this is your attempt to engage in conversation. I will stop you right now.

Your attention is neither wanted nor needed. I would never risk my career or license. So, if you would please step out of my way, I can continue with I what I am required to do." Without another word, Saint steps aside.

Demon is walking in with Gabi in the baby carrier and Gavin on his hip. The air in the room is electric. Sofia is the first to look away and side steps Demon, with the fast-clicking heels fading towards the front door, ending with the click of the door shutting quietly behind her. Demon watches her go, then turns back to the crew. Then I see something I have only seen a handful of times in my days with Demon. A grin.

Vi rushes to take Gabi. Gavin is struggling to get to his mother. "Food is getting cold," Saint says, scraping back his chair to sit down.

A room filled with everyone who means something to me, except for Risk. His chair is empty. War is seeing what I'm seeing. "He left early last night, and he isn't here this morning," War states the obvious. "Any guesses?"

I shovel a fork in mouth, swallow and shrug my shoulders. "Looks to me like the gazelle is running, and the lion is in pursuit."

Vi looks at me confused. "What?"

"Hanna." That says it all.

"Really?!" she squeaks in excitement. "I love Hanna."

"We all love Hanna," Maddie and Ava state.

"Maybe, just maybe, we should let them figure it out," I tell them. The men agree. The women, well I can tell that this is not going to end here.

CHEAP SHOT, DAD

We spend the day with family. Even Risk makes a cameo appearance. He swings Gavin around and tickles him until he is exhausted. He snuggles with Gabriella and reads her a story to lull her to sleep. It's time to head home.

I get a call from Sofia Donati later that night. "Mr. Moore, I received a call from your father's lawyer. They are shocked by the turn in the case. I wanted to warn you that your father may be placing a call directly to you. I wanted to counsel you to refrain from negotiation without my presence," she advises.

"Got it," I say simply. On cue, the phone rings directly as I hang up with Sofia. I check the caller ID and see that it's my father.

"Yeah," I answer. Ian Moore was not pleasant in my younger years and now he has confirmed that he is even more of a prick in his old age.

"Is that any way to greet me?" he scolds.

"I have been informed not to speak to you. I am going to hang up now," I state.

"Wait. Your mother would be deeply ashamed over your and Nathan's actions," he taunts.

"Stop right there. You have no right to speak about my mother at all. My mother was a loving woman who believed in family. She wanted Nate and me to be happy. Being happy doesn't mean we do as you say. It means following our own path. Shame on you for trying to use my mother's memory this way. You disgust me. That's a cheap shot, even for you Dad." I slam the button to end the call. I am resisting the urge to hurl the phone across the room.

I turn to do just that and see Vi leaning against the doorway. "I'm sorry honey," she says quietly.

"This is not on you, Vi."

"I'm sorry that this is happening to you and Nate. This must be bringing up old memories." She walks to me and wraps her arms around my waist. "It's going to be okay, Bear."

"Yeah, this I know. What irks me is that he decides to use my mom's memory against us." I clasp her closer, pressing her cheek against my chest.

"Let's go to bed. I'll help you make better memories to think about."

"Careful what you promise," I tease her. She pushes back. Undoing the belt of her silky pink robe, she allows the robe to fall from her creamy shoulders, accentuating the pink silk teddy that scarcely reaches her ass. The sight of her silk thighs, smooth skin, and kissable mouth is all it takes. She struts past me, raking her fingers over my chest. I watch her sway her hips, pausing before glancing over her shoulder.

"Coming, honey?" she asks, enticing me seductively.

"On the bed. Just as you are, on all fours, pretty girl." My girl wants to play? We can play.

CHAPTER 25

Hanna

One kiss. It was only one kiss. Why can't I forget it? That night, he took me home because my soon to be ex-husband trashed my car. I was upset, he was consoling me, and we kissed. I jolted out of the car and ran into my home, never looking back. That was the end.

Well not really. He comes into my shop, orders, sits, eats, pays, and leaves. I drop off goodies at the club house and he helps me unload, exchanges pleasantries, and disappears. He is trying to be friends. I just don't know if I can do that. It was only one kiss, but I can't forget how soft his lips were. Firm, full lips pressed against mine. His hands on either side of my face, tilting my head slightly to deepen our kiss.

It was the best damn kiss I had ever had.

Then my ex holds Vi and I hostage. I am grateful he didn't touch Vi. I would never forgive myself. My decision to marry a man capable of such violence should not have affected my friends. I am stunned that they still consider me as such.

With my idea to take Vi in until she and Orion could work things out, I knew it was only a matter of time.

Allan had been trying to regain my attention for some time. I had ignored him. Ignored his calls, emails, letters, even to the point of turning and walking down another street to avoid him. He took matters into his own hands and decided to teach me a lesson. I am not a stranger to his tactics. I've been hit, slapped, and kicked by this man who professed to love me. It wasn't until I was stabbed twice and left on our kitchen floor to fend for myself while he went out to cool off that I managed to crawl to my cellphone and call my brother. I've called the police so often in the past, but his family had too much power in this town and my cries for help went unheard.

I thought that was the end of his reign of terror. I was wrong.

I woke in a hospital room with Risk by my side. I feigned sleep because I could not face him. I am not worthy of someone like him. Only beautiful women like Ava, Maddie, and Vi can have those men. I get the Allans. So, I choose to be alone. If only I could forget that kiss.

CHAPTER 26

They don't leave

Guard

A sheet of thick bullet proof glass separates two chairs placed opposite one another. A phone on the wall is our method of communication. The iron door opens and allows Ghost to enter. He sits down on the chair and I follow suit. His bald head is tattooed in a Celtic warrior design. His eyes are steely grey and cold. He is as big as Orion. Huge in fact. Deadly, to most. Brother to me.

He lifts the phone and taps it on the glass to indicate that I do the same.

"You alright?" I ask.

He nods.

"Do you need anything?"

"Yeah, the regular. I can use it for trade," he utters.

"Orion is getting married," I tell him.

"Shit. Good for him." He nods again. "Sweet piece."

"Perfect for him. Orion wants you to meet Vi and Gabi." I come here often and have kept him informed about the goings on in the club.

"Soon."

"When?" I have been waiting for word on his return for what seems eternity.

"Soon," he repeats. "What do you need?" he continues to ask.

"Inmate 95784. Almost killed his ex-wife. Held Vi hostage. Beat the shit out of his wife for years. Stabbed her and left her for dead," I inform him.

"Right," is his only response.

"Inmate 94981 attacked our women. Almost killed Vi," I say. "War and Orion will do what they need to do if it comes to that."

"They don't leave," he confirms.

"Not if it costs you. I want you home," I tell him.

"No blowback," he responds.

"I want you home," I repeat.

"They don't leave."

"Right." I sigh. I drop my head to gaze at the table in front of me. How do I reach him? Ghost knocks on the glass to get my attention.

"Be. Home. Soon." He accentuates each word. His eyes tell me everything I need to know. Now I nod.

He places the phone back on its hook, turns to the bars and walks away. I watch him carefully. Every moment, motion is a sign. He places his hands behind his back as he waits for the guard to let him back into the jail. He signs the phrase, *Sooner than you know*.

THEY DON'T LEAVE

I take a deep breath. Good, he needs to come back to us.

I walk to my bike. War, Orion, and Risk and are waiting for me. Their shades are directed right at me. We are clad in Satan's Pride jackets, motorcycle boots, jeans, and t-shirts. We when ride together, uniformity is the key. They are trying to decipher my mood.

Weeks ago, my men sat me down, needing a plan to ensure their women will never live in fear. On both occasions the cops showed before we could exert our own retribution. Prison is penance, death is justice. Men like Jeffery and Alan prey on women. The impact of the tyranny Maddie, Vi and Hanna faced by these men has not been forgotten. Maddie and Vi have the love of their men. Their confidence has been restored. They are better than they have ever been. Hanna is a work in progress. Risk is having difficulty deciding on his approach, if any. His inner demon is staking his claim. We're hoping Hanna is the one he'll fight for.

I hop on my bike, slap on the helmet, and rev the motor. I say the next words loud enough that they can hear. "Done. Plan's in motion. We ride."

Nothing touches us. I guard our club.

CHAPTER 27

The Wedding

Orion

The women have done a great job transforming the compound into a wedding venue. I stepped back from the planning and let Vi have her dream wedding. It was her decision to have it here. Furniture has been moved; chairs all dressed in white are set up in rows. Each row is decorated with wildflowers on the ends in Vi's favorite colours of lilac, pink, and white. They added crystal drop lighting in and around the room. At one end, a platform is set with flowers, again set in the same hues as the others. This is where we become husband and wife.

I reflect on my past. I have made so many errors in judgement. I stopped believing that I merited happiness. I wanted this for all my brothers, yet never saw myself in love again with a woman giving me all of who she is unconditionally. I thought Lisa was the only woman I would ever love and allowed her memory to be a reason I stopped moving forward. In reality, it was the fear of losing someone I love again.

There were only two conditions I put in place for the wedding. The first was writing our own vows. The second was not asking my brothers to wear monkey suits. On the second we had to negotiate. No suits, but we were wearing dress slacks and crisp white shirts. Casual chic, she calls it. And, the Satan's Pride jackets are only worn after pictures. I can live with that. The only one that gave me an annoying grunt was Demon.

Vi insists that it is bad luck to see the wedding dress and bride before the wedding. She's holed up in my room here at the compound, getting ready. Gabriella has been hanging with Dad and his boys. Gavin has become very protective of Gabi. Wherever she goes, Gavin seems to follow. Gavin is full on running at this point and is giving Ava and Guard a run for their money. He is a curious kid. Just a few minutes ago, Maddie came to collect Gabriella to get her dressed to be the flower girl for this shindig. She walked away with Gabriella on a hip and Gavin taking her hand and walking up the stairs. Maddie looks good holding a baby. I'm not the only one who thinks so; War is following her with his eyes as she disappears from our sight.

On the other end of the room is a row of tables, all dressed in white lace linen with a shimmer of pale pink. The caterers arrived an hour ago and are doing setup. Cream plates and silver cutlery, crystal glasses, everything that my future Mrs. Moore wants. Beside

THE WEDDING

the food tables is Hanna. We enlisted her to create a sweet and candle table. She also made the wedding cake. Hanna has set up tiered platters with a dessert to please every guest here today. On the top of her list were, you guessed it, lemon bars. The three-tiered cake consisted of different flavours. The main tier is chocolate, because who doesn't love chocolate. The second was is new flavour that she calls apple spice. The top tier is lemon-lime. The icing is cream and pale pink with the same wildflower theme. Vi will love it. Nearby stands Risk, watching from a distance. A few nights ago, I saw him lingering in an alley where he had a solid view of Hanna's bakery. He stays until she shuts everything down and the lights go out, then roars his bike to life and leaves.

Our guests are in for some surprises. Most look at the building structure and think they are walking into a warehouse; Vi created a flawless wedding venue. All the brothers are in attendance. Those with old ladies and children are welcome as well. Nate will be coming with a heavily pregnant wife. Emily and Vi have become very close over the last few months. Vi was tense when asking me about inviting her mother and Aaron. I have to admit that Aaron has been more than considerate in driving Marie to our place at any time so that they can bond with Gabriella. He has also looked after Marie, making sure that she has the best care. Marie is his everything and with Marie comes Vi and our family, so I see Aaron embracing the change.

I refused to send my father an invitation. That was the only real argument that come from this event. Vi explained how important family was and was afraid that I would regret my actions if I didn't try to reconcile with my dad. I flat out refused. This led Vi to send a letter of her own to Dad, explaining that he is missing out on the beauty of a grandchild and another on the way. She pleaded for him to reconsider his position and accept that his sons have the right to their own choices and as parents our roles are to love and guide them. The result of this letter was a legal call from Sofia informing me that if Vi sends another letter to my father, he will be suing us for harassment. Needless to say, I blew my stack. Once I calmed myself down, we sat down and discussed the situation. I shared that although I was unsure of her relationship with Aaron and Marie, it was important to her and therefore, I made it a priority to me. I expected that same courtesy. She apologized and then she got rip roaring mad at my father for accusing her of harassment. The only way I got her off that kick was to get her in bed and fuck the anger out of her. I had her orgasm three times that night, letting her sleep so soundly she forgot the situation altogether.

Guard approaches. "Go time, man. You ready?" he smirks.

"You trying to talk me out of it?" I tease.

"Not a chance; best idea I ever had was marrying Ava. There is nothing like having a woman by your side, encouraging you, believing in you," he says.

"You're right about that."

"The reverend is waiting at the altar. I am going up to get your bride to be, while you get in place. Hanna is walking around, getting the guests to take their places. You might want to see if you can pry Nate away from his wife. He is one nervous father to be," he laughs.

THE WEDDING

I laugh along with him. Nate has been a little nutty since he found out about the baby. He bought a pregnancy book to read cover to cover and now he's constantly checking in with Emily and she's about to lose her mind. Nate takes her coffee, checks her meat to make sure it's well cooked, and threw out every sushi takeout menu.

"I better get Nate before Emily files for divorce then." I laugh.

Vi had chosen Ava to be her matron of honor. She asked Maddie and Hanna to stand with her as her bridesmaids. I figured this was going to happen, but when we talked about it, I could see Vi was holding something back. She schooled her features, but I can always tell when she isn't saying what's on her mind.

"Babe, spill it," I prodded.

"No, nothing." Yet, her eyes didn't not move from the ever so intoxicating view of her teacup. She had already dropped three teaspoons of sugar into and had been stirring non-stop for ten minutes.

I stopped her hand from stirring, placed her hand between the two of mine. "Eyes, pretty girl." Vi slowly shifted her eyes to me. "There is nothing we can't figure out. We talk it out. Baby nothing can be that bad. Just say it," I said soothingly.

I could see her take a deep breath. "I want Guard to give me away." I stop and blink. I have to say this came as a surprise for me. I thought she would want her mother, or maybe to even walk down the aisle on her own. I motion to say something when Vi interrupts me.

"I don't want Aaron for obvious reasons and although we are working on it, it just doesn't feel right. Mom hasn't been a mom in so long and again, it doesn't feel right. I considered walking in by myself. Truth is that Guard gave me something that day when we had that fight about you only coming after me because of the baby. He gave me the truth of how I let you close yourself off. That day he empowered me to take our love back. I was afraid to share and he opened my eyes. I know that he is who you want for your best man and if that's what you really want, then I can walk in alone," she finished.

I had no idea that they'd spoken that night. What is apparent is the impact of their conversation and how that talk opened the gates for our communication.

"Guard will be honored. I already spoke with Guard and he knows how important it is to me to have him and Nate stand with me. Guard is going to love walking you in on his arm, then he can come to stand by us both," I tell her.

"You think he'll say yes?" she asks excitedly. I nod and chuckle. Crisis averted.

I walk to Nate, who is on his haunches, talking to Emily's stomach.

"Mind if I take him away for a while?" I ask Emily.

"Please do, then maybe I can go steal a crab puff because if Nate is around, he will certainly stop me," she teases.

"No fish. Too much mercury," Nate responds in a serious tone.

I kiss Emily on the cheek and whisper, "I'll send one over." Her eyes light up and her smile deepens.

"Let's go, Nate. Need my brother by my side." I clasp my hand on his shoulder and direct him to the altar.

THE WEDDING

Everyone is in place. War, Risk, and Nate are by my side. The music begins and the guests move their gaze in the direction of the aisle. Hanna is leading the way with Gavin and Gabriella in a wagon. Gavin is sitting behind Gabriella, his legs open wide, holding her steady so that she doesn't bounce around. Hanna is wearing a pale purple dress with a deep vee and empire waist. She looks pretty even though she's avoiding eye contact. She keeps looking back to the kids to make sure they are still in place. Her trail ends and she picks up Gabriella and brings her over to me where she gleefully exclaims, "Dada," stretching her arms out for me to take her. Hanna then takes Gavin out and walks him over to Risk, who takes his hand. Risks looks at Hanna like she's one of her delectable desserts. Hanna doesn't make eye contact and quickly motions to remove the wagon from the center of the aisle.

Maddie is next; her long flowing hair gorgeous above her one shoulder lilac dress which cascades to the floor. She glances around the room, but her eyes meet War's like no one else exists. Ava follows suit in her regal, royal purple gown in a sweetheart cut. Her hair is up and away from her heart-shaped face. She sees little Gavin waving wildly at her and she waves a little wave and giggles at her boy.

The guests stand and face the aisle. Guard steps forward and stretches out his hand. Vi walks out and places her arm in his. She is blindingly beautiful. Her dress reminds me of a Hollywood starlet's, full length cream silk, tailored to her body, emphasizing her breasts, small waist, and hips. The dress is a halter style and her headpiece is the likeness of a roaring twenties band that wraps around her head with her simple styled dark hair making it stand out even more. No veil, she told me. Vi has always said she wanted to keep it simple. She is holding her wildflowers and is breathtaking.

Guard leads her to me. One arm is holding our daughter I extend the other for her take. Handing her flowers to Ava, she takes my hand and join us at the altar.

As we exchange rings, I say these words to her: "I searched a lifetime to feel whole. Thinking I had it all when I met my brothers, to discover I was still hollow. I had hole that I thought would never be filled. Maybe because I didn't deserve it, I feared. Then you came and you made me feel all the wonder that is you and I ran. I ran because I couldn't bare for you to wake up one day and wonder why you settled for a man like me. I pushed you away, before you could push me out. Each day without you, I was condemned by the memories of our time together. I was lucky to have been given a second chance with you. I will spend all my days showing you how much I love you. I will never give you cause to believe that you are not the most important part of my life, along with Gabriella. You are not only the mother of my child; you are my destiny. This is who we are meant to be, together. I vow to you all that I am, and all that I can become." Emotion clogs my throat with my last words because I feel so much for this woman. I slide the ring on her finger. I created the design for her. A platinum band surrounded by rubies and diamonds to match her engagement ring.

A single tear falls down her cheek. She grips my hand firmly. She clears her throat and reaches for the ring being held by Guard.

"You are the most loyal man I have ever known. There is no show, no façade, no judgement in who you

THE WEDDING

are. Your brothers respect you. Their families trust you. Our friends and family believe in you. You are all those things to all those people. My man, the only other soul that speaks to mine. Gavin, as a given name, Orion as an earned right. The hunter that you are. You hunt for truth, peace, and honor. You have taught me to speak my truth, even when I am unsure of the outcome. You will teach Gabi and any other children we may have what a true man needs to be to protect his family. My vow is to stand by your side, to assist you in creating the world we choose, and to teach our children how to be the best form of who they can become. I love you." Vi's eyes are glistening with tears. She slides the ring on my finger.

Gabriella is becoming impatient in my arms when the reverend announces us husband and wife. I kiss my bride passionately, forgetting that the room is filled with family and friends. Gabi lets out a loud squawk, pulling us apart and making the entire room erupt with laughter.

The party is a huge success. We eat, drink and laugh into the night. It's past midnight before I am able to steal my wife away to a cabin about an hour out of town. We both agreed to stay close by in case Gabriella needs us. Maddie and War are staying at our place and looking after her until we get back. Vi changed into jeans and motorcycle boots along with me, hopped on my motorcycle and we rode off into the night. Vi clung tight, her arms wrapped around my waist. An hour with Vi enveloped around me, warm air blowing in our faces. Every time I look over my shoulder to check on her, she blinds me with a beaming smile.

CHAPTER 28

The Ring

Vi

My first night with my husband. I shouldn't be nervous. Orion and I have been lovers for years. For goodness sake, we have a daughter together. And for some insane reason, here I am in the bathroom, primping myself to look beautiful for my husband. I'm nervous. Not about the sex because I know how well we connect sexually. Orion, my Bear, my man, my life.

After one last glance in the mirror, I peruse my reflection. After three lingerie shops, I found a cream lace nightie that came just above my knee. The slim lace straps covering my shoulders and tight bodice enhance my full perky breasts, making me feel sexy.

Orion is sitting up in bed, with the covers up to

his waist. His bare chest and firm shoulders are a magnificent sight. He holds out his hand. I walk over with a little bounce in my gait, taking his hand. He leads me in arranging my legs on other side of his, facing him.

I take his ring hand and circle the ring with my finger. His gaze follows my finger.

"You know I made this ring myself," I tell him.

"It's beautiful, Vi," he says in his smooth, mellow voice.

"Thank you. Did you see the design?" I ask. I lift his hand and ring higher, so that he can get a closer look.

"Is that a shield and club?" he asks.

"Yes, it is the sign of Orion the hunter. The club represents your protection of Gabriella, me, the Pride, and those who mean something to you. The shield represents the control you own over your emotions. In the midst of chaos, I can count on you to make the best decisions for our family. I chose a black ring made of tungsten carbide and titanium. They are the strongest of metals. Strong like you. You have overcome and rebuilt, and I am in awe of all that you are. I am so proud of you, Orion," I say huskily.

His hands frame my face, his thumbs stroke along my cheekbones. His eyes are blaring heat, his lips loose over mine. At first the kiss is soft and gentle, but then it deepens. His mouth is ravaging mine, tasting and savoring. My hand clenches his hair. I am desperate for more of him. He returns my passion by whipping me onto my back on the bed, continuing to feast on my mouth.

He wrenches his head back. Sliding the straps of the nightie down, baring my breasts in the process. He takes one pebbled nipple in his mouth and bites lightly, making me whimper, the fingers of his other hand rolling and pulling the other nipple. He feasts like a starving man. I tremble with need.

"More," I plead.

He catches the lace in his hands and tears open the nightie to reveal the tiny triangle thong. His mouth traces the path to the scrap of lace between my thighs. Warm kisses and licks all the way to the hem of my panties. Suddenly, Orion flips me onto my stomach and lifts my knees, planting them in the bed. His hands and lips discover every crevice of my backside. His fingers sensually massaging, his lips kiss the back of my thighs and over my cheeks. His thumbs hook under my thong; he slowly drags it down to my knees, then pulls my legs apart as far as they'll go with the thong in place. His hand on my back places me lower with my arms stretched out before me, grasping the pillow.

"That's my good girl," I hear, immediately followed by his mouth on my pussy, lapping up my juices. His fingers separate my pussy lips and I feel one finger enter me while he continues to suckle my clit. My hand clenches the pillow and I am moaning loudly. I hardly recognize my own voice begging, "Don't stop, baby. Please don't stop."

He adds another finger and quickens his pace. I want to spread my legs further apart, however my panties are in the way. His torturous mouth licks the seam of my pussy. Over and over. I am going to die of frustration at this point.

I find myself flipped onto my back, my legs straight up, panties tossed aside. "Play with your tits, pretty girl. I want to see you play." I comply immediately.

His sudden thrust takes my breath away. His jaw is clenched, and he is showing great restraint. "Fuck, Vi. You feel so good. Tight, hot, wet." He moans.

"Fuck me, Orion," I say, panting. He moves inside me and he is going hard and fast.

"Tell me if it's too much," he groans.

"More, bear. Don't stop." I am going to die if he stops now. His hands on my ankles spread my legs wide. He is mesmerized as he watches his cock slide in deep, each stroke harder than the last. I'm on the brink. My stomach clenches and my muscles tense. I grip his cock with my pussy. My fingers gripping the sheets, my head moves side to side, and I fall over the edge of the cliff into a primal oblivion of ecstasy.

My grizzly bear doesn't stop. He continues to plow into me until I hear him roar. God, he is beautiful. Wild, crazed with need, and glorious. Eventually, we calm our breaths. Orion pulls me close to his chest and throws a sheet over us both. He takes my ring hand in his and places them on his stomach. Our fingers intertwined, his breathing deepens, and his eyes shut into a sweet blissful sleep.

This is my forever. We know it won't be perfect. There is always a new challenge over the horizon. It's fine. I have his back, he has mine, and Satan's Pride stands strong.

The End

About the Author

A.G. KIRKHAM knows romance! Born in one of the most romantic countries in the world, Italy! Her family migrated to Canada when she was a young girl, and she quickly fell in love with reading and writing. Her favorite time in school was getting lost in the books. Th at feeling has never left. And she has been writing short stories and poems from an early age. Her world is fi lled with off -beat friends and family who make her life zany and unique—all the better for enhancing the creativity in her work! She was always the "good" girl growing up, but somewhere along the way her "rebel' girl has emerged in her books and in life. She is the author of the popular Satan's Pride series including Guard, and now War, where each book represents the belief that love truly exists!

Follow her book series at www.romancebyagkirkham.com

Playlist for Orion's Book

Sweet Home Alabama - Lynyrd Skynyrd
Sweet Child of Mine—Guns N' Roses
Fall to Pieces—The Script
Look How God Made Her—Thomas Rhett
Bruises—Lewis Capaldi
Nice to Meet Ya—Nial Horan
Tequila - Dan & Shay
Fight—Tyla Parx Featuring Florida Georgia Line
Play with Fire - Nico Santos
Beautiful Crazy—Luke Combs
Let It Go—James Bay
Speechless—Dan & Shay
Bones - Maren Morris
Simple Man - Lynyrd Skynyrd
South of the Border—Ed Sheeran & Camilla Cabello
10,000 Hours—Dan & Shay Featuring Justin Bieber
Take me to Church—Hozier
Perfect—Ed Sheeran